Love Isn't a Show

Emily Walters

Love Isn't a Show

Published by Emily Walters

Copyright © 2019 by Emily Walters

ISBN 978-1-07532-515-1

First printing, 2019

All rights reserved. No part of this book may be reproduced in any form or by any electronic or mechanical means including information storage and retrieval systems – except in the case of brief quotations in articles or reviews – without the permission in writing from its publisher, Emily Walters.

www.EmilyWaltersBooks.com

PRINTED IN THE UNITED STATES OF AMERICA

Dedication

I want to dedicate this book to my beloved husband, who makes every day in my life worthwhile. Thank you for believing in me when nobody else does, giving me encouragement when I need it the most, and loving me simply for being myself.

Table of Contents

CHAPTER 1 1

CHAPTER 2 10

CHAPTER 3 17

CHAPTER 4 25

CHAPTER 5 33

CHAPTER 6 40

CHAPTER 7 44

CHAPTER 8 49

CHAPTER 9 61

CHAPTER 10 68

CHAPTER 11 76

CHAPTER 12 81

CHAPTER 13 89

CHAPTER 14 97

CHAPTER 15 107

CHAPTER 16 113

CHAPTER 17 118

EPILOGUE	123
WHAT TO READ NEXT?	126
ABOUT EMILY WALTERS	129
ONE LAST THING...	130

Chapter 1

Kristen Manning pushed the "end" button on her phone. She wanted to sing and shout and dance around her tiny apartment. But instead, she stood frozen in shock, her phone still clutched in her right hand. As soon as she gathered her wits, with shaking fingers, she dialed her mom's number.

"MOM! I have the best news!" she exclaimed into the phone when her mother picked up the line.

"What is it, sweetie?" her mom asked.

"You know how I sent an audition tape to that show, *Dance With Me*?"

"I think I remember you telling me about that a while back."

"Well, I just got a call from the show's casting director! I've been selected to compete this upcoming season!" Kristen squealed, jumping up and down, although she was alone.

"That's great, honey. So that means what?" her clueless mother prompted on the other end of the line.

Kristen sighed in exasperation, forgetting that her mother watched little television outside of the evening news and reruns of *I Love Lucy*.

"It means that in two weeks, I'll be traveling to LA, meeting my famous dance partner and competing live on television for a chance to win a huge trophy and $100,000! Mom! This is so exciting! I can't believe they picked me!"

"I can believe it. You're beautiful, smart, sweet and funny. Why wouldn't they pick you?"

"You're my mom, you have to say that," Kristen joked as she walked around her apartment with excited energy coursing through her veins.

"What about school though?"

"I only have a couple semesters left before I finish my master's. I'm just going to take this upcoming semester off. It won't put me behind schedule all that much, and besides, there's no way I can miss this amazing opportunity!"

When Kristen hung up from the chat with her mother, she surveyed her tiny apartment a couple of blocks from the Auburn University campus. She'd called this place, humble though it was, home since her junior year of college. Now that she was just two semesters away from completing her master's degree in fine arts, it was hard to believe her time there was nearly over. She had worked in the university's theater department as a teaching assistant for the last year, and she hoped to find a permanent position in the department once she finished her studies.

Love Isn't a Show

She loved the stage—either being on it or behind the scenes, which was one reason she'd sent in an audition tape for *Dance With Me*. She had little ballroom dance experience, but that wasn't a problem. The whole point of the show was to pair regular, everyday people with professional ballroom dancers and see their transformations as they became dancers themselves. Seeing as her career goals involved performing, or teaching others the art of performing, it seemed like a good idea to audition. Kristen hadn't actually believed she would be selected though. She was just a graduate student from Alabama. Nothing necessarily special.

She wondered who her partner would be. Most of the male ballroom dancers on the show were quite handsome. Two weeks couldn't pass by fast enough! Kristen glanced at the pale pink calendar hanging on the front of her fridge. She had so much to do before she left. Classes to rearrange, a meeting with her adviser, shopping for new workout wear for practices, as well as cute outfits in case she had a chance to get out and about in Los Angeles, not to mention packing enough clothing and accessories for a potential three-month stay alone was a major feat.

Flipping open her computer, she quickly searched on YouTube for past videos of the show. Within seconds, several clips popped up on the main page. Many featured the heartthrob and superstar of the show, Ansel Stavros. With his devilish good looks, to die for body, and moves like nobody's business, she could see why he was a favorite with the show's fans.

Kristen admired his moves as she watched the video of him performing a quickstep with a rather agile partner, but she rolled her eyes as she glanced at the news articles popping up in the sidebar about him. He was always dating a new girl, and unfortunately, he had a never-ending supply from which to choose. Women were always throwing themselves at him. Kristen had also read somewhere that he was notorious for hooking up with his dance partners on the show, as well.

"Please don't pair me with him. Pair me with any of the other guys, just not Ansel Stavros," she whispered under her breath as she skimmed through the articles.

***

Two weeks and one day later, Kristen entered an overly air-conditioned dance studio in West Hollywood wearing her new harem pants and mint green yoga top. She'd pulled her light brown hair into a carefully constructed messy bun on top of her head.

"Hi there, I'm Ansel Stavros, your partner for the seventh season of *Dance With Me,*" the too handsome man with glossy dark hair and deep brown eyes said, stepping forward to close the distance between them. Kristen's eyes grew wide as a camera crew surrounded her. The initial meeting between partners was always

Love Isn't a Show

taped, but she was floored to find out that Ansel was her partner, and had a hard time immediately smoothing her face into a pleasing expression, even if there was a chance millions of viewers would see the footage next Tuesday night.

"Kristen Manning," she replied mechanically, sticking out her hand in greeting.

He smiled and winked. "I don't shake hands, I hug," he informed her, scooping her into a hearty embrace and lifting her off the ground before she knew what was happening. As he spun her around, her mind was still reeling that the one guy, *the one guy,* she had prayed she wouldn't end up with as a partner, was now, in fact, just that.

"We're going to have such a blast together, Kristen," Ansel told her once he'd set her feet back on the floor.

"I'm ready to get started and learn all that I can," she said, not quite meeting his eyes. She willed herself to shake off her surprise and disappointment.

"Is something the matter?"

"No, nothing's wrong," she replied brightly, putting a smile in place for the cameras circling around them.

"You seem a little tense." Ansel extended his hands to her. "Why don't we go through a few basic steps and loosen up a little?"

Kristen swallowed. Despite her personal determination to not be affected by this guy, she certainly could understand his massive appeal. In his strong, sinewy arms, with his dark eyes intent upon her, it was impossible not to be attracted to him.

He leaned in. "Mmm. Your hair smells so good," he remarked. "Like vanilla and coconut."

She stepped away from him, laughing awkwardly, her hands subconsciously touching her blond-streaked tresses. "Thanks."

He smiled tenderly. "You are most welcome. Now, shall we dance?" he asked, extending his hand to her. Hesitating only a brief second, Kristen slipped her hand into his. Ansel was a good leader, guiding her through simple steps as she grew accustomed to being in his arms.

"You have natural grace. Have you danced ballroom before?" he asked as he whirled her about the room.

"I'm getting my master's in fine arts, so I've been in a few musicals that required a bit of choreography, but other than that, no, I've never really danced before," she told him, the words spilling fast and nervous from her mouth.

He chuckled, his eyes staring deeply into her, to her very core. She felt vulnerable, exposed at his gaze. "Well, you're a natural, which makes my job a lot easier," he confided.

Love Isn't a Show

"Thanks," she said, blushing. Mortified, she couldn't believe he affected her like this. She didn't want to be affected by him. He had a reputation.

After they'd practiced for a while, he told her they were done for the day. "That's all?" she asked. Kristen had expected to be there for several hours.

"The first day of practice is more or less a meet and greet," he said with a shrug. "Now that I know what you are capable of, I'll choreograph a routine and we'll get started on it first thing in the morning."

"Oh, okay."

"Kristen?"

"Yes?" She looked up from where she knelt gathering her gym bag and water bottle.

"Would you like to have dinner with me tonight?"

She stared at him. "I-I I don't think that's a good idea," she stammered.

"Why not?" he asked, his face blank.

"Well . . . I just don't think it would be a good idea," she repeated.

He stepped closer to her. "Is it because you've heard things about me?"

Her head shot up. "What? Oh, no! No, not at all," she lied, her face turning red.

He gave her a knowing look. "I only ask you to dinner because I think it would be good for us to get to know one another better, especially since we will be working closely for the next three months. If you've heard rumors about me, they aren't true."

"I guess we could go to dinner then," she relented, weighing her options in her head. The frozen meal in her temporary apartment's freezer didn't seem all that appealing, and it wouldn't hurt to get out and experience a bit of LA with a native. She would simply keep her distance from him. Ansel may just have told her that the rumors about him weren't true, but she highly doubted his words. She'd have to stay on guard.

"Great," he smiled at her, his bright, white teeth contrasting against his tanned skin.

"What's your number?" he asked, pulling out his phone and typing it in as she relayed it. Her phone immediately vibrated in her hand.

"I just texted you, now send me your address, and I'll pick you up around seven."

"I can just meet you at the restaurant," she offered.

"I don't mind swinging by and picking you up. Parking can be a headache around here."

"Okay," she said, typing in her address and texting it to him.

Love Isn't a Show

"Your apartment isn't far from mine," he said, glancing at his phone.

"Yeah, the show has a sort of deal with that building. The apartments are small, but really nice, and contestants can stay for free while they are competing," she told him. "But you already knew that, didn't you?"

"I didn't know all the details. I figured that was probably where you were living."

She gathered up her stuff. "I should be going now."

"See you at seven, then?" he asked with a wink as he walked out the door.

"At seven," she nodded with a slight wave, her insides flopping around with excitement or fear, she wasn't sure.

Chapter 2

She'd taken more care getting ready for her dinner with Ansel than she wanted to admit. It had taken her well over an hour to settle on an outfit, and her bed in the studio apartment was covered with a mound of discarded shirts, dresses and skirts. She finally settled on an emerald green swing dress that made her blue-green eyes pop, and managed to smooth her blond-streaked hair into submission. Slipping into a pair of buff ankle boots, she surveyed her reflection in the mirror, satisfied with the results.

As she spritzed the air and walked through a cloud of her Kate Spade perfume, letting it settle onto her skin, the doorbell rang. Butterflies immediately filled her stomach. Grabbing her patent leather clutch and her cellphone, she ran, nearly tripping over the corner of the rug in front of the sofa, to answer the door. Before she turned the handle, she took a deep breath to calm herself. It was just a casual dinner with an acquaintance, she reminded herself. No need to get so worked up.

Swinging the door open, she had to remind herself to breathe at the sight of him. Dressed in vintage jeans and a simple black T-shirt that allowed the perfect glimpse of his muscled arms, Ansel stood smiling at her. His dark, tousled hair and even darker eyes exuded sexiness, and the scent of his subtle, spicy cologne drifted toward her.

"Hi," she finally managed to say.

"Hello, Kristen," he said, his voice husky and smooth. "Ready to go?"

She nodded, stepping into the hall and locking the apartment door. Ansel slipped his arm around her, causing her to freeze up at the close contact.

"Oh, hey sorry, I guess you didn't know dancers are extremely touchy-feely. It's in our nature. Sorry," he explained, removing his arm and placing it back by his side as they walked to the elevator.

"It's okay. Something I'll have to get used to, I guess," she offered.

He shook his head as they stepped inside the elevator. "I don't want to make you uncomfortable. It's second nature for me, but not for you. I'll try to keep my hands to myself," he said with a wink.

She laughed. "No, it's okay. You don't have to be anything but yourself. Don't feel like you have to tiptoe around me. If we want to do great in this competition, we have to get comfortable with one another," she heard herself say. It didn't seem that keeping her guard up would be all that easy of a task.

"You're right, Kristen. We have to get to know each other, develop a natural chemistry, which I don't think we'll have much of a problem doing," he told her, leaning in as if he were divulging a trusted secret. A shiver ran down her spine, and it certainly wasn't rooted in fear. No, desire was coursing through her veins as she felt the warmth of his breath on her neck, his lips near her ear. How was she ever going to spend the next three months trying to keep herself physically separated from him?

She cleared her throat, trying to break the spell that had so quickly been cast. "Where are we going for dinner?"

"Lucques. It isn't too far from here, and the food is amazing. It also has a nice patio that I thought you might like."

"Sounds wonderful," she said as they walked into the parking garage beneath the building. He placed a light hand on the small of her back as he led her to his sleek, silver Mercedes. He helped her into the passenger side of the two-seater.

They rode in silence to the understated restaurant. When they arrived, they were ushered right inside to a private table on the covered patio. Kristen noticed that Ansel was recognized by nearly everyone. It just then sank in that she was out in LA with a celebrity. Up until that moment, she'd known Ansel was certainly the most popular pro on the show, but she hadn't realized how famous he truly was.

She bit her lip, overwhelmed as he held her chair out for her. Would she be featured on TMZ that night?

"They'll stop looking in about two minutes," he whispered in her ear before taking his seat across from her.

"I don't think I realized how . . . popular . . . you are," she said slowly.

"I try not to think about it. If I do, it weirds me out a little," he said as he glanced over the wine menu. "Do you have a preference?" he asked, gesturing to the list.

"I like dry whites or sweet reds," she told him.

"We'll have whatever you suggest that is either," Ansel glanced at Kristen, "a dry white or a sweet red," he told the waiter when he appeared.

"I know just the thing," the waiter said before disappearing.

"So tell me about yourself," Kristen said after she'd looked over the menu and decided what to order. The braised short ribs sounded appetizing.

Before Ansel could answer, the waiter appeared again and poured their wine. Ansel waited for Kristen to approve the cold, crisp white wine, which of course, she did. They also placed their orders before the waiter left them once more.

"What would you like to know?" Ansel asked, picking up their conversation.

"Where are you from? What do you like to do?" Kristen started.

"My family is originally from Kranidi, a city in Greece, but my grandparents migrated to California in the fifties. They owned, and now my father owns a sailboat manufacturing company."

"Interesting. Do you like to sail?" she asked.

"How could I not like to sail? It's in my blood. What about you? You're from Alabama, right?"

"Yep. How could you tell?"

"Well, once you open your mouth, no one could mistake that you're from the South, but I read it in the summary I was given."

"You were given a summary about me?"

"Once we meet our partners for the season, we're given a little information sheet. Just highlights."

"Oh? What did you learn from this informational sheet?"

"That you're 22, getting your master's, and that you've wanted to ballroom dance ever since you watched Fred and Ginger in *Top Hat* when you were ten years old."

Kristen's mouth popped open. "A little invasive, don't you think? I get them telling you the first two facts, but my love for Fred and Ginger Astaire is another thing altogether."

Love Isn't a Show

Ansel laughed. "They want us to get to know our partners."

"How long have you been dancing, might I ask?"

"I started ballroom dancing lessons as a child, as my mother pretty much forced me and my two brothers to take them. She said we needed a little refining. Once I realized I was pretty good at it, I started competing. Mainly so I could dance with girls," he said with a wink.

"Ha, ha. Very funny," Kristen replied.

"No, that's the truth. I had no idea it would take me here, to this place. But I do love it, and I think that's what's most important. That you love what you do," he said seriously.

"That's why I'm getting my degree in fine arts. I don't expect to be a famous actress or celebrity. I just love the stage, the expression, the art of it all. I want to share that love with others—whether it's performing or teaching others to perform."

"That's admirable."

"Thanks," she said as his gaze intensified and she warmed beneath it. She took a sip of her wine, but that did nothing but fan the flames growing within her. Why, oh why, did he have to affect her like this?

Their food arrived and as they ate, they swapped stories of their childhoods before falling into a comfortable silence. Kristen was thankful for the break—it gave her a chance to gather her thoughts and settle down from the effects of Ansel's inescapable charm. She thought she was in the clear, until they were waiting for the valet to bring his car around.

"So, do you want to come over to my place for a drink?" Ansel asked, slipping his hand into hers.

"Yes," she replied without thinking.

Chapter 3

"Are you going to get out?" Ansel's voice startled Kristen from where she still sat in the passenger seat of his car. She looked up at him and his offered hand.

"Yes! Sorry, I spaced out for a second," she said, shaking her head as he helped her from the car.

"Would you like me to take you home, Kristen? I will, if you're uncomfortable. I promise, you have no reason to worry though. I respect you, and I only invited you here to have a drink in a more relaxed setting. We were having such a good time getting to know one another, I'm not ready for it to end yet," he told her as they took the stairs to his second-floor loft apartment.

"I'm not ready for it to end yet either," she admitted.

Ansel unlocked his door and held it open for her. She stepped into his apartment, which was much cozier than she expected. She'd fully anticipated seeing the epitome of a bachelor pad—black leather couches, modern art and a sterile coolness. Instead, the loft with its exposed brick walls held a gallery of family photos, Oriental rugs offered understated luxury on top of the concrete floors, and a comfy-looking sofa was situated in front of a gas fireplace. A rustic table sat in front of a large bank of windows, and the open kitchen was rather inviting with a few plants on the counter and a kettle on the stove. The place looked homey and cheerful. Not at all what she expected.

"Would you prefer coffee, tea, or something a little stronger?" he asked as he shut the door behind them and led the way to the kitchen.

"Anything is fine," she replied, following tentatively behind him.

"How about an Irish coffee?"

"That sounds good to me," she agreed as he started making them.

Once he'd made their drinks with Kristen watching, they settled on the opposite ends of the sofa, a fire in front of them, no other lights on in the house, save for the recessed lighting beneath the kitchen cabinets.

"You know, I've never immediately clicked with a partner the way I'm clicking with you," he said, his eyes mesmerizing in the firelight.

Kristen took a sip of the strong drink before setting it down on the cocktail table. "I've never had a dance partner before, so I can't return the sentiment."

Ansel laughed. "You're so funny, Kristen," he said, setting his cup beside hers and scooting closer and tucking a strand of hair behind her ear, "and smart and beautiful, and when you laugh, your nose crinkles and your eyes practically dance." By the time he finished his sentiment, his voice was a throaty whisper. Her eyes were locked with his, not a trace of a smile left on her lips. The tiniest bit of resolve she'd been clinging to up until that point faded completely away. All she could think about was if it was possible to mentally will his lips to touch hers.

Ansel drew closer, until he was leaning into her, his lips hovering close to her own. She couldn't think, couldn't breathe. When his lips grazed over hers, soft and tender, she melted into him, wrapping her arms around his neck. He returned her passionate embrace, his kiss intensifying. She couldn't get enough of him, desperation for more of the feelings he stirred within her, desire and passion and electricity she'd never experienced before, driving her to throw caution to the wind.

A deep moan escaped her lips as Ansel's hand traveled up her bare thigh, slowly making his way beneath her dress. His mouth traveled down her neck, the heat of his lips branding her as he nipped and kissed. Kristen's hands reached beneath his shirt, and he paused momentarily to help her rid him of it, tossing it carelessly to the floor. She surveyed the muscled planes of his chest and the chiseled hardness of his abs, swiftly flicking her own dress over her head and throwing it down before he leaned down to devour her with his kisses once more.

His hands roamed down the length of her mostly bared skin, cupping her breasts, covered only by the sheer lace of her bra. His thumbs rubbed against the lace, teasing her nipples into tight peaks. She watched as his eyes dilated with lust for her—this man, who could have anyone he wanted, wanted her—she was driving him crazy. She could see it in his eyes. The look of devilish desire alone made her suck in her breath, arch her breasts into his hands.

Ansel leaned down and trailed kisses along the cleft of her breasts, the soft swells peeking over the edge of her skimpy bra. But he didn't stop there, he continued down the center of her body until he was pressing kisses along the band of her sheer panties. Her pulse pounded, her body throbbed. She resisted the urge to arch her hips more than necessary as his fingertips skimmed over the tops of her legs, hooking into the silky band and easing her panties over her hips, past her thighs. He slowly, painstakingly slid them down the rest of her legs.

He deftly removed his own pants as she lay there, mostly naked, save for her bra that concealed nothing, panting as his eyes raked over her. She'd never craved a man's touch like she did right then. So desperate with need, if he didn't touch her soon, she would do it herself.

"You're so beautiful," he murmured as he came down over her, kissing her neck as his hand slipped between her legs. She cried out at the sheer bliss of his touch, and his mouth captured the sound.

"I want you," she whispered, positioning herself against him, feeling the heat and hardness of his cock pressing against her. She didn't want to wait a second longer.

He groaned, seeming to want her as badly as she wanted him, even if he was trying to relish and linger in the moment. Despite the inner battle he seemed to be having, within seconds, he was inside of her, thrusting powerfully. Her legs wrapped around his waist as she took him in, moaning in ecstasy.

Despite the initial zeal, he slowed up, moving gently as her hips rocked in rhythm with his own. He reached between them, massaging her as he slid in and out, the intensity building as his thrusts grew more powerful until he rode her to the edge, her mind and body shattering into pieces as she cried out in pleasure. His rhythm became even faster, more erratic, until barely a moment later, she held him tight as he came.

They lay in a tangled heap, a shimmer of sweat covering them both as they tried to catch their breaths. Her arms and legs felt languid, her eyes half closed. After a few moments, he kissed her forehead, smiling gently down at her, and reality slowly began to sink in. She'd only known him for less than a day and they'd just had sex.

She struggled to sit up, grabbing her dress off the floor and tossing it quickly over her head. "I don't know what got into me—I don't do things like this," she said nervously.

He took her hand in his, never losing his calm demeanor. "Hey, it's okay. Calm down. We have a long journey together, and we clearly have natural chemistry."

"Even so, we shouldn't have done that," she told him honestly. "Sex complicates things." He wrapped his arm around her.

"I don't know about you, but I have real feelings going on here," he said. "Something about knowing we'll be working together for a while—it feels good."

She shook her head, the cold reality of who she had just slept with hitting hard. He was a renowned playboy. He spoke a smooth game—so smooth she'd had sex with him the day they met even though she knew about his reputation beforehand.

"Look. Ansel. I really want to focus on this competition, and I had a great time tonight, but it can't happen again. Can we just be friends?" She didn't want to get hurt, and if she let herself fall for him, that's exactly what would happen.

"Of course," he smiled.

"Can you take me home now?"

Love Isn't a Show

"Sure, but if you want to stay the night, you're more than welcome to do so," he said, trailing his hand on her bare knee.

She shot up from the sofa. "No, thank you though. I need to get a good night's sleep for rehearsals."

"Yeah, we'll be working together most of the day. Let me get dressed real quick and I'll take you home," he said, hopping up and heading to his bedroom. She made a point not to watch, instead, she focused on gathering her shoes and unmentionables.

***

Kristen rubbed her eyes as she glanced at the clock in the dance studio. Although she'd arrived back at her apartment before midnight, she'd tossed and turned, unable to sleep. Now, anxiety filled her being as she waited for Ansel to arrive for rehearsals. He was two minutes late. She took a sip of her soy latte. Was he late because he was uncertain about seeing her after what had happened the night before? Was he going to request a new partner?

She nervously paced in front of the wall of mirrors, catching a glimpse of her blond-streaked hair and apricot workout leggings from time to time. Maybe she should text him. See what was keeping him.

Ten minutes later, he waltzed in, coffee cup in hand, all smiles. "Good morning, sorry I'm late!"

"No problem," she said as the camera crew fiddled with their cameras and mics. They were going to tape a segment of them rehearsing today. "Did you come up with something for our first dance?" she asked, biting her nail.

"Of course," he said smoothly as he dropped his bag on the bench. "We were assigned the salsa, so I've put together a spicy number to a song called 'Fireball.' Have you heard it before?"

"Sure, it was pretty popular last summer, wasn't it?"

"Yep. Anyway, it has great rhythm and a strong Latin vibe."

"Okay, well I'm ready to get started whenever you are," she said cheerfully. She inwardly sighed with relief as she followed him to the center of the room. They were acting like nothing had happened the night before and she couldn't have been happier. It seemed like the previous night's events were going to be easily and swiftly swept under the rug. But then he started showing her the dance moves, and everything changed.

Chapter 4

The days leading up to their first televised competition waffled between manic exhilaration and extreme exhaustion. Throwing in the palpable desire emanating between Ansel and her every time he pulled her into his arms and led her through their salsa routine, no wonder, by the time she waited backstage at the live taping on the following Tuesday evening, she was wound tighter than a girdle on a Baptist minister's wife at an all-you-can-eat pancake contest. She giggled as that particular quote, courtesy of Blanche from *The Golden Girls*, popped into her thoughts. As she smiled, she clenched the handrail along the walkway, reminding her that it still made it no less true.

She took a slow, deep breath, closing her eyes as she exhaled. Everything would be fine. They would do fine. Ansel had told her that she was nailing the routine—that there was no way they would be eliminated next week in the first round. She just had to get through this week without freezing up or tripping and falling flat on her face.

Glancing in the direction of the makeup tables and hair stylists, she caught sight of Ansel where he sat patiently as his face was dusted with stage makeup, and her heart warmed. She couldn't help it. Even though she knew it was dangerous to develop feelings for him, they slammed through her like a freight train.

But when she watched him stand, walk over and sidle up next to one of the troupe dancers, all smiles as he slipped an arm around her and whispered in her ear, the freight train of warm, fuzzy feelings took a downward plunge off a cliff, and was quickly replaced by anger. She swallowed it down. They were just friends. She'd insisted that they were just friends. She had no right to be mad at him for flirting with other girls. That was the type of guy that he was, which meant that he was certainly not boyfriend material.

Kristen pushed off the wall and headed to the balcony that overlooked the dance floor, unable to watch him in action any longer. Surveying the busy studio, currently filling with a live audience as crew members bustled across the floor, she took it all in—it was hard to believe she was there, on *Dance With Me*, less than an hour away from performing live with Ansel Stavros of all people. It was also hard to believe she'd slept with the heartthrob less than a week ago. She shook her head at all of the surreal changes to her life in such a short time.

"Hey, you," his warm, lilting voice cascaded over her shoulder, close to her ear. She momentarily closed her eyes and basked in the sound before the image of him whispering in another dancer's ear popped into her mind. Her back straightened.

"Hi," she said shortly.

"Nervous?" he asked, standing beside her, their shoulders touching.

"A little," she replied.

"Is everything okay? You seem sort of mad at me," he said, turning to face her. She stayed facing forward, her eyes not leaving the activity taking place below them.

"I'm fine."

"In the detailed history of mankind, I'm pretty sure no woman that has ever said she is fine, is actually, in fact, fine. What's wrong?"

"Nothing, Ansel. I'm just a little nervous."

He slid his arm around her, leaning close to her cheek as he whispered, "Remember Kristen, this dance is all about passion, spice and heat. You can't be mad at me for whatever reasons you're not telling me, unless you're going to channel those feelings into a sultry, sexually charged kind of anger."

She turned to face him, unable to keep her anger in check. "I think I can handle that," she said hotly, her teeth clenched.

He smiled in amusement at her response, fanning the flames of anger within her. "Just go away, right now," she said quietly.

"Your wish is my command, but here's a tip—when the cameras start rolling, don't look so pissed at me. It's not good for votes. Act like you and I are . . . you know, really into each other. Which in my defense, you're the one that shut that down."

She rolled her eyes. "Got it. I just need a moment to clear my head. Get in the game," she told him. She was a professional. She'd taken numerous acting and drama classes. She had natural rhythm. She could pull this off.

"Okay, but you need to meet me in the green room in ten minutes," he told her before walking away.

***

Forty-five minutes later, after their names and the dance style they were performing were announced over the loudspeaker, Kristen stepped saucily towards Ansel in her sparkling red high heels, her glittering dress in reds, oranges and golds resembling fire as the lights played off the sequins. As the music pulsed through the studio, he grabbed her passionately and they spent the next two minutes executing their salsa routine to perfection. She channeled the anger she felt towards him into her movements, her gaze intense.

For anyone watching who didn't know any better, the two of them looked to be in a battle of longing and desire, heat and lust radiating from their movements. To finish the dance with a flourish,

Love Isn't a Show

Ansel spun her into their final turn before dipping her low over his leg, holding her tightly into his arms with his eyes locked on hers, searing through her soul. Momentarily, her defenses melted away, and she returned the intense gaze of desire, but then the crowd broke into wild applause and the spell was broken.

The three professional judges praised them on their chemistry, techniques and the difficult choreography she'd managed to perfect for the first week of the competition. When Ansel and Kristen ran backstage, hand in hand, it was impossible for her to hide her elation as they made their way to her dressing room, needing a moment to calm down after the dance. Water bottles and towels had been carefully laid out for the two of them.

She jumped into his arms. "AHH! I'm so happy right now!"

He held her tightly, whirling her around. "You did amazing! Amazing! I'm blown away!"

"Thank you," she said sincerely, leaning back to meet his eyes.

He smiled down at her. "You are most welcome," he said, and he leaned down and kissed her before she could protest.

Riding the high of their performance, she didn't stop him. His lips melted against hers as his hands roamed up and down her back. Her fingers tangled in his hair as the kiss deepened. She knew she shouldn't have let him kiss her, but that didn't mean she didn't want him desperately. Just as his hands dipped low to cup her bottom, pulling her so tight against him, she could feel his own desire for her, a rapid knock at the door sent them scrambling apart.

"Just a minute," she called out shakily. She straightened her costume as Ansel grabbed a water bottle and took a seat on the small sofa.

"Yes?" she asked, opening the door with a polite smile in place. A crew member in a black T-shirt, wearing a headset, stood on the other side.

"Just needed to let you and Ansel know that you're expected for a follow-up interview in ten minutes."

Kristen gave the guy a thumbs-up and another sugary smile. "Got it," she said before closing the door and whipping around to face a grinning Ansel.

"Stop looking at me like that," she demanded now that her brain was thinking clearly again.

"Like what?" he asked, faking cluelessness.

"Like you've seen me naked."

"I have seen you naked."

"But you're not going to see me like that again," Kristen informed him.

Ansel laughed. "Okay, sure."

Love Isn't a Show

"What's that supposed to mean?" she asked in exasperation.

"You say you don't want me, but your eyes, your lips, your body . . . says something very different," he pointed out.

She crossed her arms across her chest, the sequins on her dress scratching against her forearms. She scowled at him.

He raised his hands in defense. "Look, I don't know why you keep denying your feelings. I have feelings for you, too. What's so wrong about that?"

"The only part of you that has feelings for me needs to stay in your pants," she seethed. "I know about you, Ansel. Not just what's written in the tabloids, but what I've seen with my own eyes. Sure, you might think you feel something for me, but that doesn't stop you from feeling something for every attractive female within your range."

"I'm charming, I can't help it."

"That's your defense? Really?"

He stood from the sofa and raked his hands through his hair. "I don't know what you want me to say. Yes, I have a thing for you, but no, I'm not interested in making a commitment, settling down, blah, blah, blah."

She rolled her eyes. "I never said anything about a serious commitment. We work together every day. We've slept together. How do you think it would make me feel if we were having sex all the time, seeing each other every day and I still had to watch you attempt to stick your tongue down half the troupe's throat?"

"IF we were sleeping together all the time, I wouldn't flirt in front of you. Or behind you. Or whatever."

"How can I believe that?"

He shrugged and walked towards the door. "The fact is, you don't want to try anything. You're scared, and that's fine. Just stop being so pissed at me. It's not good for our partnership." Finishing his final argument, he walked out and firmly shut the door behind him.

Chapter 5

The next three weeks passed in a whirlwind of sequins, spray tans and hairspray. Ansel and Kristen led the pack for the first two weeks with their breakout performance of the salsa on premiere night, followed by week two's intricate hip-hop routine with popping and locking and even a bit of isolation. Coming into the third week, they were gearing up for a much more elegant, intimate rhumba to an Ed Sheeran song for their weekly Sunday night live performance.

"This is a lot harder than I thought it would be," Kristen said, breathing hard as she mopped her face with a towel. The afternoon sun streamed into the dance studio as the romantic song filled the space.

"Everyone thinks the slower dances are easier, but they actually require more control, more intensity," Ansel said before taking a big gulp of water.

"And a lot more physical contact," Kristen remarked. As they'd practiced the dance, she found her resolve melting as Ansel held her close, his hand trailing intimately along the inside of her arm, down her waist. When she wrapped her arms around his neck as he pulled her fast across the floor, the tips of her toes gliding across the glossy floor, she nearly fainted. From overwhelming feelings, or from the fact that it was really hot in the studio that afternoon, she wasn't sure.

"Are you feeling alright, Kristen? You look really tired," Ansel remarked as he restarted the music and reached for her hand.

"I'm fine, just a bit more tired than usual. I guess this schedule we're keeping is starting to catch up with me."

They went through the routine a few more times, but on the final run-through of the day, when he dragged her across the floor, the last thing she remembered was the tight embrace of his arms as he caught her before she hit the floor.

***

"KRISTEN! Kristen, wake up! Are you okay?" Ansel's voice broke through the fogginess of her mind. She struggled to hold on to what was going on. Her eyes blinked open to see him leaning over her. She attempted to sit up, but he shook his head at her.

"I called the medic and they'll be here in just a second. Are you alright? You fainted a few minutes ago while we were practicing," he explained, his face etched with worry.

Thank goodness, she'd only been out a few minutes, she thought to herself as she glanced around. "I think I'm fine. I must have gotten overheated."

Love Isn't a Show

"I still want the medics to check you out before we continue."

"Can I at least sit up? I promise, I'm fine," she told him.

He nodded, extending a hand to help her into a sitting position. She waved it off, rising on her own. She really did feel fine.

A few minutes later, two paramedics, dressed in navy blue, bustled into the studio carrying a large black bag. They helped her into a chair, took her blood pressure, checked her heart rate and listened to her breathing.

"You seem to be in good health. Have you had any fainting or dizzy spells before today?" one of the paramedics, an older woman with a ponytail, asked her.

Kristen shrugged. "Nope. I really think I just got overheated."

"Have you ever overheated before?"

"No, but I've also never been practicing dance routines for hours on end every day either."

"We feel comfortable letting you resume practice today, but take it easy, okay? If you start feeling too warm or out of breath, take a break," the medic told her, then glanced at Ansel. "Make sure she takes care of herself, alright?"

"Absolutely," Ansel said with a nod.

Once they left, Kristen stood up. "Okay, let's get back to it."

Ansel shook his head. "Nope. We've practiced enough for today. I want you to go home and relax, okay?"

Kristen huffed. "You're kidding me, right? We have at least another two hours of studio time."

"Well, that doesn't really do us any good if you pass out again. You look really tired. As your partner and instructor, I think it's best if you go home and rest."

"Fine," she snapped. Grabbing her bag, she stormed from the studio, tears burning her eyes. When she reached the parking lot, she sat in her rental car for a few minutes as the irrational, angry tears flowed down her cheeks.

"What is wrong with me?" she asked to the empty car. First fainting like a weakling in the middle of practice, then snapping at Ansel, and now crying for no apparent reason in her car. Thinking through the possibilities, she figured that it must be PMS. She was supposed to have started the week before, but assumed that the strenuous exercise as of late had shocked her body and thrown her off schedule.

Gathering control of herself, she cranked up her car and left the studio. No use trying to talk to Ansel right now. It was best to just do what he said and go home, rest and hope that she felt better the next day.

When a firm knock echoed on her apartment door a couple of hours later, she peeled herself off the sofa to see who it was. Opening the door, she stared at Ansel in confusion.

"What are you doing here?" she blurted out.

"I didn't want you to be mad at me. So I brought you dinner and a movie," he said with a sigh, lifting his hands, one holding a plastic bag, the aroma of Chinese takeout wafting deliciously from its contents, and the other holding a couple of Redbox rentals.

She continued to stare at him blankly. "Why are you being so nice? Don't you have better things to do?" she asked, but moved aside to let him to enter the apartment.

Ansel shrugged. "I know you think I'm a bad guy, but you're my partner . . . and my friend. I sent you home, and I was worried about you. Is that such a crime? Besides, I brought my apology in the form of sweet and sour pork and romantic comedies I would never be caught dead watching under any other circumstance."

Kristen folded her arms across her chest, enjoying watching him squirm just a little too much. "Okay, fine. Thank you. I'm over it, anyway, and I think I actually owe you an apology—I overreacted."

Ansel carried the food and movies over to her small dining table and dropped them. "We're good now, right? So, no worries."

Kristen picked up a takeout box and a pair of chopsticks. "Don't you have better things to do tonight than babysit your partner? I'm sure you have a line of women jumping for a chance to be seen with you."

"Yes," he said matter-of-factly, prompting an eye roll from Kristen, "but I'd rather be here right now. Is that such a big deal?"

She swallowed a mouthful of noodles under his intense gaze. "I guess not," she stammered, but her insides flip-flopped. They ate, sitting on the sofa after Kristen popped in one of the movies he'd brought.

"Thanks for coming over," she said begrudgingly, her defenses lowered. It really was such a sweet and thoughtful, though unexpected, gesture, on his part.

He leaned toward her as the movie blared in the background. "I know you don't believe me, but I really think there's something between us," he murmured, his voice low and husky.

She sucked in a sharp breath. She knew he thought that about nearly every female he met. That was his way. But as he closed the inches between them, kissing her lips tenderly, she let herself forget. His

Love Isn't a Show

hand tangled in her hair, his mouth warm against hers.

After a couple of minutes, she pulled back. "I don't know about this," she said tentatively.

"I do. I like you, Kristen, a lot," he whispered before pulling her against him. She didn't protest, finally giving in again to the overpowering chemistry that had charged between them since day one. As he carried her to the bed, she vaguely remembered promising herself she wouldn't let this happen again, but as his mouth captured hers as he lowered her onto the soft, gray coverlet, she closed her eyes and blocked out everything except the way he made her feel in that moment. In her darkened apartment with the warmth of his bare skin against hers, the rest of the moments didn't seem to matter all that much.

Chapter 6

Kristen bolted upright in her bed the next day as the early morning sun streamed through the cracks of the blinds. She barely noticed the sleeping figure next to her, the sheet slung low at his waist, his bare, muscled chest rising and falling in deep slumber, as she flew out of the bed, almost tripping over her running shoes lying haphazardly at the foot of her bed in her hurry to get to the bathroom.

After she finished throwing up, she sunk to the tiled floor, feeling miserable. She hated throwing up—her head pounded and tears slipped down her cheeks involuntarily. However, the last thing she wanted was for Ansel to find her naked and crying on her bathroom floor. She initially struggled to rise, but managed to wash her face, brush her teeth and rinse out her mouth twice for good measure before slinking stealthily back to bed. Ansel still slept, unaware that she'd gotten sick.

After slipping back under the covers, she lay on her side, facing away from him, just in case she had something contagious. She felt fine now, though. Maybe the Chinese food hadn't agreed with her. She tried to fall back asleep, but in the light of the day, the implications of her night with Ansel weighed too heavy on her mind.

Love Isn't a Show

Where they just fooling around? Did he really have feelings for her? How would this affect their partnership?

She sighed in frustration.

"You think too much," the low, throaty voice from the other side of the bed interrupted her silent reverie.

"Well, there's lots to think about," she countered. "Good morning to you, too," she added.

Ansel chuckled, and reached out to pull her close. "I need to ask—if I didn't have real feelings for you, do you think I would have stayed the night?"

She turned around to face him and his eyes grew wide. "Are you okay?" he asked before she had a chance to speak.

Briefly closing her eyes, she answered, "Yeah, I'm fine. I'm guessing the takeout didn't agree with me, but I feel perfect now, I promise."

"Your face is a little swollen," he said, reaching out and gently stroking her cheek.

"I know, but I feel fine now. Ready to get the day started," she replied, scrambling from his embrace and heading to the bathroom. "I'm jumping in the shower. We're due at the studio at nine. There's coffee in the kitchen if you want to make some."

Ansel sat up. "Actually, I better run home to change and shower. We don't have much time." He slipped on his jeans and jogged over to where Kristen's head still poked out of the bathroom door. He planted a quick kiss on her lips. "See you later," he said softly before she shut the door.

***

Ansel checked the time later that morning at the studio. Kristen wasn't one to normally run late. He smiled to himself as a memory of their night together popped into his mind. He supposed he had thrown her off her morning routine. He rubbed his chin. It really wasn't like him to stay over at a woman's place. But over the past few weeks, the more he'd gotten to know Kristen, he really liked being around her.

Sure, their first night together, he'd been attracted to her, but it wasn't the way he was attracted to her now. This was new territory for him. He wasn't one to have feelings like this. He'd been genuinely concerned about her the day before, and had gone to her apartment with no intention of sleeping with her. He'd only wanted to hang out, but sitting so close to her, watching her eyes dance when she laughed at the movie, her full lips curl into a pout when he teased her at the sappy scenes . . . well, he just couldn't help but kiss her. And she'd certainly kissed him back.

Now that it was twelve hours later, a satisfying twelve hours later that had encompassed them making love twice, although it would've been three times if she hadn't looked like she didn't feel well that morning, he wasn't sure where they stood. This was new territory for him. Sure, he'd hooked up with almost all of his dance partners—even the married one—but this was different. Those hookups had only been about the physical gratification. He'd NEVER stayed over with any of them, and he wouldn't have classified any of them as friends. Kristen was different somehow. He couldn't explain how, but she was.

Just then, she bustled into the studio, dropping her bag and water bottle. She looked fresh and energized, a far cry from the way she'd appeared this morning. The messy knot of blond-streaked hair on top of her head bounced with every step she took, and her tanned skin glowed against the hot pink workout pants she wore. Her lips were seashell pink, ever so slightly glossed, and her blue-green eyes were bright and excited when she saw him.

"Good morning," he said as the crew started filming. "Again," he whispered in her ear as he gave her a friendly hug in greeting. She blushed, and he stifled a laugh.

"Why don't we just get started?" she asked, trying to seem like she was all business, but she peered at him conspiratorially with those blue-green eyes of hers.

"Sounds good to me," he told her, switching seamlessly from lover to partner/coach mode.

Chapter 7

Two weeks later on a Monday morning after their first slip in the competition, Kristen's eyes welled with tears. However, her tears weren't related to anything regarding her dancing. She squeezed her eyes shut, refusing to believe the truth staring up at her from the bathroom counter. This was the last thing in the world she needed right now. She shook her head as a sob slipped out.

"Kristen?" Her eyes darted to the closed bathroom door. "Look, I know we were in the bottom three couples last night, but that's no big deal. Mambos are hard to execute. We can rally and get back on track this week. I don't think we have to worry about being eliminated," Ansel's voice carried through the door.

She wished she was only upset about the possibility of being eliminated in the competition. Finishing up the fifth week of competition in danger of being voted off didn't seem like all that big of a deal with a positive pregnancy test sitting on her countertop.

"Just go away," she said, her voice cracking. Everything had been going so well between her and Ansel the past couple of weeks. She actually thought they might have been developing into something sort of real. She thought back to that first time, when like idiots, they hadn't used protection. She didn't know what she'd been thinking. She was normally so careful! They always used it now. Just that first time . . . way back at Ansel's apartment.

"Is that what you want? For me to leave?" His voice sounded hurt, even muffled through the door as it was.

"Yes," she lied, her voice breaking.

"I don't believe you."

"Does it matter? I just need a little time. I'll meet you at practice later," she told him.

She didn't hear anything for a moment, but then he sighed loudly. "Okay. I'll give you some space. I'll see you in a couple of hours," he said.

Kristen put her head in her hands and sobbed once she knew he had left.

***

She was late again. Ansel glanced at his watch, wondering why she'd texted him to meet her at a coffee shop around the corner from the studio. She knew how important it was that they spend every bit of their studio time practicing.

When he'd left her apartment that morning with her still locked in the bathroom, he was worried. But now? Having him meet her somewhere other than the studio? He was on high alert. What if she wanted to drop out of the competition? Had the intense pressure gotten to her?

He drummed his fingers against the outdoor bistro table, full of nervous energy. Just as he was about to flag the waitress down and switch his espresso for something decaf, he caught sight of her walking towards him. His heart fell to his stomach at the sight of her usually bright blue-green eyes full of worry and concern . . . and something resembling utterly devastation that he did not like at all. She wore a black sweatshirt and leggings, her hair in a ponytail, her face free of makeup. She somehow managed to look effortlessly beautiful, even when she looked to be in the midst of personal crisis.

"What's wrong?" he asked as soon as she took a seat across from him.

Kristen bit her lip, a fresh spate of tears welling in her eyes. "Everything," she said, her voice thick with emotion.

He reached out and took her hand. "Talk to me, Kristen."

"I don't know how to tell you this," she said with difficulty.

A thousand scenarios ran through his mind. Was she sick? Was she leaving to return to Alabama? Had someone died? "Just say something. You're really scaring me," he admitted.

"Because I'm scared myself." She stared at the table.

He said nothing, only waited for her to continue with whatever it was she needed to get off of her chest.

"Ansel, I'm pregnant," she said quietly, glancing up at him to see how he would react.

He stared at her.

"Wait, what?" he said in confusion. He must have heard her wrong.

"I'm pregnant," she repeated.

"That can't be possible. We're careful."

"Actually, if you remember, the first time, we weren't," she reminded him. He thought back to that first night—he'd been so enamored with her, the look of her, the feel of her beneath his hands—he'd meant to grab a condom from his bedroom but everything had transpired on his sofa so quickly.

"Are you sure?" he asked, still unable to believe what he was hearing.

"I took a test this morning."

"Well, take another one," he replied. This couldn't be happening. This didn't happen to people like him.

"O-Okay?" She responded, her voice trembling. He couldn't take it. He couldn't have this conversation right now—it was more than he could handle. Shooting up from his chair, he turned to leave.

"Ansel?" He heard her voice, small and frightened. "Are we practicing today?"

He turned, shook his head, and walked away, knowing it was the worst thing he could have done, but he did it anyway.

Chapter 8

Kristen chugged the Gatorade in her hand and stared at the four pregnancy tests lined up on her counter. So far she was four for four. She'd bought one of every brand the drugstore down the street from her apartment carried. Three more to go. Hence, the Gatorade.

Even as she drank the lemon-lime, electrolyte-laden concoction, she knew she was doing it in vain. She was pregnant, and there was no doubt about it. She had all the symptoms, she'd missed her period and she'd had morning sickness already for crying out loud. But something about watching Ansel walk away had sent her fleeing to the drugstore and raiding the family planning aisle.

What was she going to do? This really wasn't something she was prepared to handle. She didn't think calling her parents or any of her friends in Alabama with this news was such a good idea. It needed to be kept a secret for as long as possible. She wanted, no she needed, to win this competition. Babies weren't cheap, and of course, she was keeping it. There was no doubt for her about that matter.

Her hand drifted to her flat stomach, the thought of a little life growing inside of her completely unfathomable. But even if she couldn't believe it, it was there growing nevertheless, and it was her baby. Her and Ansel's child. She rubbed her temples. There was so much to do, so many conversations to have, but she figured the most important step she needed to take next was to see a doctor and get the pregnancy officially confirmed, make sure everything with the baby was okay, and ensure that continuing to dance wouldn't be an issue.

With one fell swoop, she slid the tests into the bathroom trashcan, deciding to take the other three tests at a later time. Right now, she needed to find a good obstetrician in Los Angeles. Pulling out her phone, one quick Google search later, she dialed the office of Dr. Cathy Goldblum, who had excellent reviews online and also took her insurance.

The first available appointment they could offer was two days away, smack dab in the middle of her and Ansel's scheduled rehearsal time. She took it though, knowing how important it was to get this whole pregnancy thing officially confirmed. She quickly texted Ansel after hanging up with the doctor's office.

Kristen: Hey, just wanted to let you know that I have a doctor's appointment Friday at eleven. Could we reschedule our practice?

She waited patiently for Ansel to respond, but it was a solid twenty minutes before she heard her phone chirp, alerting her that she had a text message. Not like she was clutching it in her hand or anything.

Ansel: Fine. I'll see what I can do.

Kristen: Is that all you have to say?

Ansel: I don't know what you want me to say. This isn't something I was prepared to hear. Just make sure it's official, okay? Then, we'll talk.

Kristen: Fine, but are we rehearsing tomorrow?

Ansel: Yes, we're going to have to rehearse. Otherwise, there's no way we'll be ready for the quickstep Sunday night.

Kristen: I guess I'll see you tomorrow then.

Ansel: Yeah.

Kristen tossed her phone on the sofa beside her and sighed in frustration. She knew this was a massive curveball for the both of them, but did he have to be such a closed-off jerk about it? She dreaded the idea of seeing him the next day, but there was no way out of it. Baby on the way or not, they were still dance partners.

***

The next morning, Kristen woke up with a knot of apprehension in her stomach. With bleary eyes and no caffeine, she showered and dressed for rehearsals, forcing one foot in front of the other. Having to pretend everything was okay in front of the cameras was going to be no easy task.

With her hair in a fishtail braid and a coat of mascara on her lashes to liven up her sleepy eyes, she drove to the studio in her rental car, munching on a few saltines and stopping to pick up a ginger ale from a convenience store on the way. She prayed under her breath that she would not throw up at practice— especially not when the film crew was taping.

When she pulled into the lot, Ansel's car was already there. She made a point of parking on the opposite side of the rather small lot, figuring the less contact between them, the better. For the time being, at least. She sat in her parked car for a moment, gathering courage to face the day ahead of her.

She made her way inside and trudged to their reserved studio. She could hear the music already blaring before she even reached the door. Wow, Ansel was really on the ball. Turning the metal knob on the door, she took a deep breath, closed her eyes while uttering a brief prayer, and went inside, hoping she looked way less defeated than she actually felt.

Her eyes widened at the scene before her. Ansel was hard at work, alright, but he wasn't alone. A brunette beauty whirled around the room with him, looking far too perfect for her own good. Had Ansel decided to have her *replaced*?

A flame of indignation roared through her. She stomped to the iPod dock and turned off the music with a forceful push. Twirling around as blood pounded in her temples, with her arms crossed she stared down the duo dancing as they froze in confusion.

"What is the meaning of this?" Kristen demanded, feeling her cheeks flush.

"Kristen, this is Yael. She's a part of the show's professional troupe, and she's helping me work on the choreography for our routine next week," Ansel explained. Yael waved and smiled kindly.

Kristen smiled back sheepishly. "Oh, okay. Sorry to interrupt." She tried to brush off her overreaction, hoping the camera crew wouldn't think anything of her little outburst. She hadn't even put her mic on yet, so maybe the footage would be unusable anyway.

"We were just finishing up," Ansel shrugged as Yael stepped to the side wall, grabbing her towel and water bottle from the floor while a crew member attached a mic to the inside of Kristen's tank top. She still felt a bit embarrassed about her flame of anger, which she knew was fueled by jealousy at seeing another girl in her place in Ansel's arms. She rolled her eyes at herself. He was a dancer, for crying out loud. Having a girl in his arms was part of his job and she knew that. But it hadn't kept her from wanting to freak out and make a fool of herself a minute ago. It had to be the hormones coursing through her body, because that type of jealousy was so not like her.

Once the crew member was finished with her, she wandered over to Ansel.

"Ready to get started?" she asked nervously.

"Yes, we've got a lot of work to do," he replied, holding out his hand for her. Once she was close, he murmured, "How are you feeling?"

His voice was so low she could barely hear him.

"Fine," she said too brightly, "just fine. Can't wait to get going with the quickstep!"

They started practicing the way they usually did—Ansel went through the steps slowly, over and over. "Now, you need to remember, this dance is called the quickstep for a reason, so you're going to be doing this at twice the speed," he told her as he led her through the steps. "And it's very important to keep your frame and never break hold—we'll get points docked for breaking hold."

Kristen nodded, half-listening as she struggled not to misstep. Her brain wasn't as sharp as usual. Probably due to the fact that she found out she was pregnant the day before. By the guy that was swinging her around and had yet to really talk to her about it. And they were being filmed. Anyone in her same situation would have a hard time concentrating, too.

Love Isn't a Show

"Do you need a break?" he asked softly about an hour into rehearsals.

She nodded breathlessly. "Yeah—I need to sit down for a second."

"Of course—rest for a few."

She started walking to the bench situated along the side wall and the camera crew headed into the hall to take their own break. Fumbling for the switch on her microphone, she turned it to the "off" position. Maybe Ansel and she could take just a few minutes to have a real conversation. She was dying for it.

But much to her disappointment, Ansel immediately left the room when the film crew did. She looked around the empty room glumly. Why wouldn't he just talk to her? The avoidance was driving her crazy! Even if they didn't discuss the pregnancy, just a little normal banter would be nice. She put her head in her hands, exhausted physically and mentally. Maybe she should just go home. Forget about this whole competition and try to resolve to her impending new life as a single mother.

"Hey," Ansel's quiet voice broke through her reverie. He must have snuck back into the studio while she was busy wallowing in her misery. She looked up, embarrassed at the tears welling in her eyes.

"Are you alright?" he asked.

"Yeah, just tired," she half-lied. "What's up?"

"Nothing, I was just checking on you—you seemed kind of out of it during practice."

"Well, given the circumstances, are you all that surprised?" she asked, her voice quivering.

"Is your mic on?" His voice was barely above a whisper. She shook her head.

"I know this is hard," he said slowly.

"Do you, Ansel?" she asked hotly. "It doesn't seem like anything has really changed for you. Meanwhile, I'm over here freaking out! I think I should just leave! Why don't you do us both a favor, and just forget you ever even met me?" She started crying, but before she could make a bigger fool out of herself than she already had, she rose, grabbed her bag and stormed out of the studio. She couldn't do this. She'd never been good at pretending nothing was wrong. That was part of the reason she was better behind the stage than she was on it. She briefly wondered how long it would take her to pack up and find a flight back to Alabama.

"Wait, Kristen!" Ansel called out behind her as she was rushing to the parking lot. She didn't wait for him, just made a beeline for her car, got in and peeled out of there. Tears blurred her eyes as she darted through traffic. How had she gotten into this mess? The image of Ansel, his sexy smile, dark eyes and rippled abs came to mind. Maybe she did know, but

Love Isn't a Show

still, when she'd made the decision to compete, she thought she was making a decision to change her life for the better. But now, her life was more than changing—it was in shambles all around her! What had she done?

She pulled into her apartment's parking deck, parked, threw her arms on the steering wheel and sobbed. She needed to go back home and try to sort out what would now be her life. She saw it stretching before her—a single mother in a dingy apartment struggling to make ends meet. She cried even harder.

A light knocking at her window startled her. She looked up, rivers of tears running down her cheeks, but she really didn't care who saw her. What did it matter anymore?

Ansel peered through the window, his face filled with concern. Sighing heavily, she opened the door and stepped out of the car.

"What do you want?" she asked darkly, trying not to sniffle like a little kid.

"I followed you to make sure you were okay," he explained, placing his hands lightly on her shoulders.

"Okay? Okay? You think I'm okay?" she asked hysterically.

"No, I don't. That's why I'm here," he said calmly. His voice sounded like honey, smooth and sweet.

"You don't have to worry about me much longer. I'm heading home—I can't do this anymore," she said, crying even harder. Ansel hesitated only a second before pulling her into his arms. She sobbed on his shoulder.

"Maybe we should go inside before anyone sees us," he murmured after a moment. She nodded solemnly, peeling herself away from him and trudging to the elevator. He slipped his arm around her.

Once inside her small apartment, she flopped despondently onto the sofa. Never before had she truly felt like her world was over the way that she did in that moment. Ansel moved stealthily about the space, and within a few minutes, she heard the tea kettle begin to whistle.

"I thought you could use some tea. My mom drinks tea when she's stressed out," Ansel said from somewhere in the kitchen.

She sat up and sniffled, watching the handsome man pour her a cup of tea. Everything about her life felt surreal. Ansel carried the steaming cup to her and she sipped from it, trying to calm her nerves.

"Do you wanna talk about this?" he asked tentatively.

She set the cup of hot tea on the coffee table. "What is there to talk about? You know what's wrong even if you won't say it out loud."

Love Isn't a Show

Ansel put his hand over hers where it rested on her knee. "You're not going through this alone, Kristen. I'm here. We're in this together."

"Are we, Ansel?"

"Of course—please don't leave. We need to figure this stuff out together. What good would come from you quitting the show?"

"Finding out I'm pregnant has been a shell-shock. It's hard to see past that right now. How can I even try to focus on dancing?"

"It's been a shock for me, too, but there's nothing we can really do at the moment about it. We can, however, keep dancing and competing."

Kristen rolled her eyes. "I figured that was the only reason you cared."

Ansel squeezed her hand. "Look at me, Kristen. I care about you more than I care about winning. If you really want to go home, you can go home—I'm not going to stop you if that's what you really want. But, you and I both worked hard to get where we are, and we're sitting solid at the top of the leaderboard. Fame aside, if we win, we both get a lot of money. Seeing as a baby is on the way, earning a large sum of money couldn't hurt anything, and that's the truth."

She nodded. He had a point. "Okay. You're right. Now, about the baby. I have a doctor's appointment tomorrow afternoon. Would you come with me?" she asked hopefully.

"I don't think that's such a good idea," he admitted, rubbing the back of his neck.

"Oh, I see," she said, a bit crushed.

"It's not because I don't want to go," he replied quickly. "I just worry about rumors starting. You and I . . . seen together at an ob-gyn's office?"

"Yeah, I guess you're right. I didn't think about that."

"What if I meet you here afterward and we can talk? Strictly about the appointment—nothing to do with dancing or the show."

She smiled. "Thank you, Ansel."

"You're welcome. Now, how about I make a dinner and Redbox run?" He kissed her softly on the lips before smiling back at her.

"Yes, perfect. Tonight, we'll relax and tomorrow we can focus on babies," she said firmly, stifling a laugh as the color drained from Ansel's tanned face.

Chapter 9

Ansel drummed his fingertips nervously on the steering wheel of his car as he waited in the parking garage of Kristen's apartment building. She was due back from her doctor's appointment any minute, and never in his life had he been so anxious. This was uncharted territory for him. He'd never had a relationship last long enough to discuss if he wanted kids, and now here he was *having a baby* with his dance partner that sure, he had feelings for, but they'd only known each other for a handful of weeks.

He ran a hand through his hair, and checked for the five hundredth time to see if Kristen's car was coming around the corner. He liked Kristen, he really did. She was sweet, funny and an all-American beauty. He really enjoyed her company, and was glad they'd actually started up something that felt so real. But a baby? *A baby*? That wasn't something he could even begin to fathom. Personally, he was freaking out at the idea of being someone's father, but there were also the repercussions of what this would do to him professionally. The network was going to be in an uproar. The producers were going to throw a fit. Knocking up your partner wouldn't necessarily be considered a good career move for him.

What was he supposed to do? He'd had enough conversations with Kristen to know that she would more than likely keep the baby. Based on her morals, religion and upbringing, that was a given. He shook his head. Why was he getting ahead of himself? She had yet to get back from the doctor. Maybe she wasn't even pregnant. Maybe it was a fluke. He tried not to get his hopes up.

He glanced up to see Kristen's car carefully pull around the corner and glide into the spot beside his. They'd felt it was best not to meet and talk about their dilemma in public, which was why he'd been waiting for her at her building. The last thing they needed was a curious fan overhearing their conversation.

Ansel jumped out of his car and met Kristen getting out of hers. She had a strange, unreadable expression on her face. She said nothing to him, only walked absently toward the elevator. He followed her, his apprehension growing by the second.

"So . . ." he ventured as they rode up to her sixth-floor studio apartment. Kristen still said nothing, so he tried again. "How did your appointment go?"

"Fine," she answered, but didn't elaborate. The elevator doors opened and she immediately got off, walking with purpose to her door. Ansel had no choice but to continue following her.

Once inside, he stood by the door as she dropped her bag and slipped off her shoes before she went to the kitchen and got a bottle of water from the fridge. It was like he wasn't even there. Ansel cleared his throat.

"Hey, look, I know you're mad at me. I get it. But could you please tell me what happened at your appointment? You're starting to freak me out!"

Kristen whirled around, her eyes wide. "You're starting to freak out? Well, buddy, fasten your seatbelt," she warned as she started rummaging in her bag. Ansel stepped over to the kitchen counter as she produced what looked like sonogram photos.

"Here, take a look at these," she said, pushing the pictures across the countertop to where he stood. He picked them up and studied them, trying to make heads or tails of what he was supposed to be seeing.

"I feel like I'm looking at abstract art. Can't you just tell me whatever it is that you're acting so weird about? I assume this is proof that there is a baby growing in there." He gestured to her general abdomen area.

"Baby?!? Try babies!" she blurted out, tugging at her ponytail, her voice a higher pitch than usual.

He studied the images a little closer. Sure enough, there were two blobs that looked nothing like babies in his opinion in the shadowy image. As realization sunk in, the photo slipped from his grasp and fell to the tiled floor. "Twins?" he finally managed to squeak out. He wanted to run. Get in his car and peel out of there to anywhere that wasn't in Kristen's apartment hearing she was pregnant with not one, but two babies. Babies, not baby. Oh, God. The room was spinning.

"Yes, twins, Ansel. Around the end of next February, I'm going to give birth to two babies." Her voice cracked. Snapping out of his own reverie, he saw the worry in her eyes. She was scared. Putting his own breakdown aside for the time being, he pulled her into his arms.

"It's going to be alright," he soothed as her shoulders slumped.

"No, it's not," she sobbed. Ansel rubbed her back. Maybe he didn't know the right words to say, but in this moment, he knew he could be there for her as she cried.

A few minutes later, she broke away from him. "Look, Ansel. This is a lot to handle, and I just feel that . . . maybe we should put any sort of romantic relationship we have together on hold. It really hurt to be walked away from when I told you about the pregnancy, and I can't deal with that kind of stuff right now. Let's just focus on getting along and getting through the rest of the competition. We're only halfway through."

Love Isn't a Show

Ansel felt like someone had punched him in the gut. Could he really blame her for putting whatever connection they had to the side right now? She was just trying to protect herself, and he wasn't even sure what was going on between them anyway. He nodded solemnly. "Is it safe for you to keep dancing?"

"Dr. Goldblum said as long as we watch the tricky lifts and are extremely cautious, I can dance for the remaining six weeks of the show. But she also reminded me that, with twins, I'll start showing a lot earlier than if I was only carrying one baby. So, by the end of the competition, I'll be about three months along, so we may have to get really creative with costuming."

"How can you think about stuff like costumes right now? You just told me we're having twins."

"Because, Ansel, if I really start dwelling on the two babies growing inside of me that have to come out of me, and then be parented by me, I am going to start crying again. It's too overwhelming. Right now, I'd like to focus on the few things that I can control, like costumes and dance practices."

"So, as far as us . . ."

"No, Ansel. I can't. Not, right now. Let's just be friends for the time being. We'd barely started dating—let's try to just get through this without messing it up any worse than we already have. And

Love Isn't a Show

I'm going to give you an out—if you don't want to be a part of this, that's fine. I understand. It's not like we planned on this happening, and I don't want to saddle you with something that you don't really want."

"I can't see you every day and pretend you aren't pregnant with my babies. I may not be perfect, but I'm not that horrible of a person. I can't pretend like I have all the answers, or even like I know what it is that I'm supposed to do, but this didn't happen to just you alone, Kristen. We're both becoming parents, and I'll support you in this—and I'll support our children, too."

Kristen shook her head. "It's not just about money, you know," she said quietly.

"I know that—I just don't know if I'm cut out to be a dad," he admitted, hanging his head in shame.

He glanced up to see her staring at the ceiling and his heart cringed as he watched her blink back the tears pooling in her eyes. "It's been a really long day. Maybe . . . maybe you should just go home now," she said, her voice trembling.

He sighed in defeat. There were at least twenty things he wanted to say—all things he probably should say—but all he did was nod instead. "I'll see you in the morning?" he asked quietly.

She bit her lip. "Yeah, sure."

Love Isn't a Show

He left her apartment. On a typical Friday night, he would have called up any of a dozen ready and willing ladies more than happy to spend the evening—and the night if he so chose—with him, but as the sun set on that particular Friday, he drove home, poured himself a stiff drink and sat listlessly on his sofa. He flipped on the television, but he couldn't have said that he was actually watching it. The noise blared, but he stared ahead, too much on his mind to even try to focus.

Chapter 10

Two days had passed since her appointment at Dr. Goldblum's office. Two days since she found out she now carried two little passengers around with her at all times. Something about that knowledge was both awe-inspiring and terrifying at the same time. And to think that Ansel was a part of that, too, never ceased to evoke an equal amount of awe and terror, as well.

Her heart still constricted when she thought about her telling Ansel that they should just be friends. Truly, it was the opposite of what she really wanted, but she'd had to say it. Otherwise, he would just keep on shattering her heart into irreparable pieces, whether he intended to do so or not. She couldn't take him freaking out on her, or having to watch him walk away from her again. She had enough to deal with as it was. And he'd pretty much told her he wasn't going to be a part of their children's lives. He'd only be willing to "support" them. She knew what that meant. Absent in every way but the check he would send every month.

But she couldn't think about that for the time being. For now, she had to dance. With him. And act, in each dance, like he hung the stars and the moon in the sky—even if doing so brought her more pain than she was willing to admit.

Ansel plopped down beside her as she watched the troupe at camera blocking for that week's live show. She shifted in her seat, tugging at her silver and black futuristic dress. "We're almost finished," he told her, handing her a bottle of water he'd grabbed for her from craft services.

"Thanks," she said as she took the water. Communication beyond absolute necessity had been pretty strained between them for the past couple of days.

"Do you want to grab something to eat after we're finished?" He nudged her arm.

She turned to him, caught off guard by his question. "Um, I guess?"

"I just think we need to work harder on our friendship, Kristen. We can't keep going like this—the audience is going to pick up on our issues with each other," he explained. She rolled her eyes. Of course, it was about the show and his precious persona. Even so, she still wanted to win, especially since she'd gone through so much in the process of getting to this point.

"Fine. I'm dying for Mexican food," she replied stiffly, looking anywhere but at him.

"I know a great, little, out-of-the-way place that serves the best guacamole I've ever tasted, but it's a bit of a drive. Why don't I follow you to your place and we can drop off your car? I promise, it's worth the effort." He flashed her his winning smile.

She sighed in mock exasperation. "Their carne asada better be good," she warned, a smile jerking at the corners of her lips.

Ansel pretended to cross his heart. "I swear, everything there is the best and authentic as you're going to get for Mexican food outside of Mexico. And their margaritas? You'll love them."

She stared at him as if he had horns growing out of the top of his head.

Realization hit him. "Oh, that's right. Sorry," he mumbled.

"It's okay. No big deal," she relented. It was an honest mistake.

"I've gotta run and go over a few details with the sound techs for our dance before we wrap for the day. Sit tight, okay?"

She nodded as he rushed off in the direction of backstage. Before she knew it, someone else had taken his place in the seat beside her.

"Trouble in paradise?"

Kristen turned to see Noah Hart, another contestant still in the competition, sitting beside her. Her brow furrowed. They'd hardly ever spoken to one another except in passing, seeing as they were competing against each other and all.

"I beg your pardon?" she asked the tall blond.

"Sorry if that came out of nowhere, but I've been watching you two, and it seems like you guys have a rather rocky relationship."

"Not that it's any of your business, but we're fine. Good friends, even," Kristen bluffed.

"I didn't mean to ruffle your feathers or anything—it's just, you know, this competition is getting intense, and I swear, my partner, Elysia, is a slave driver. I thought it might be nice to commiserate with someone in the same boat as me." He shrugged, before starting to get up, but Kristen grabbed his sequined sleeve.

"Hey, stay. You're right. This is tough and I'm sorry I was so defensive. I think this competition is making me go crazy," she told him, laughing a little.

Noah laughed, too, which showed off a charming dimple near his chin. He was handsome in a blond, blue-eyed surfer sort of way. Very outdoorsy. "So, do you regularly wear sequined shirts and sparkly pants?" she teased with a wink.

He laughed again, relaxing in the seat beside her. "No, I'm more of a khaki shorts and T-shirt kind of guy. I never thought I'd feel somewhat normal in this kind of getup, but I guess it's par for the course." He shrugged, tugging at his ice-blue shirt embroidered with silver sequins.

"I don't typically wear black leather and metallic attire to class back home," she shared with him conspiratorially, gesturing to her costume.

"So where do you go to school?"

Kristen told him about Auburn and launched into her plan to get her master's by the following spring. She was so lost in her conversation with her new friend, she didn't see Ansel return.

Ansel cleared his throat and Kristen looked up from her conversation to see him standing in front of them, arms folded across his chest, his expressing foreboding. "We're done for the day. Ready to get going?" he asked Kristen, not even glancing in Noah's direction.

She turned back to Noah. "It was nice chatting with you. We should do it again some time," she told him, patting his arm.

"Yeah, I'd like that," Noah replied with a smile and a casual wave, glancing cursorily to where Ansel stood hovering.

Ansel's eyes narrowed as Kristen rose, waved goodbye and headed to the changing rooms. He changed into his street clothes and waited for her outside of the women's changing area, then followed her silently until she reached her car. "What was that all about?" he asked finally as she opened her car door, still pretending not to notice his ridiculous jealousy.

Kristen shrugged. "I don't know what you mean. I'm starving. Can we hurry up and be on our way?"

"Fine. I'll be right behind you." Ansel turned and stomped off in the direction of his own car. Kristen slipped into her car, buckled up and pulled out of the parking lot. She wasn't even going to try and understand Ansel and his reaction to her making small talk with Noah.

***

Ansel gripped the steering wheel so tightly his knuckles turned white. Seeing Kristen chatting it up with that guy had been awful. It had taken all that was within him not to storm over there and tell that guy that he was wasting his time—that Kristen wasn't available. But then, he'd realized he had no right to do that. They were just friends. Even if she was pregnant with his babies, they were just friends. He couldn't stop her from seeing someone.

"This isn't working for me," he said as soon as she'd settled into the passenger's seat of his car and firmly shut the door.

"What are you talking about?"

"I know you said we should just be friends, but I don't think you should be dating anyone else."

"Ansel, I'm not dating anyone else, nor do I have plans to do so. But if I wanted to, I could and I would. You pretty much told me the other day that you don't even want to be a part of our children's lives. Why on earth would I care what you think about my personal life?" she asked hotly.

Ansel had started to pull out of the lot, but pulled into a spot and put the car in park again. He turned to Kristen. "Why the hell would you think that I don't want to be a part of my children's lives?"

"You said you'd 'support' them, but you didn't know if you were cut out to be a dad," she reminded him.

"Yes, I said that, and it's the truth, but that doesn't mean I'm not going to be a dad anyway. The last thing I want is for my kids to grow up not knowing their father. Of course, I'm going to be a part of their lives—even if it doesn't come easy or natural for me," he explained.

"Why didn't you say that the other day?"

"I'd just found out that you're carrying twins. TWINS, Kristen! I met you less than two months ago, and now we're having not one, but two kids together. Excuse me if I was a little flustered."

"I'd just found out the same thing, and it would have been nice for you to be a little reassuring."

"I thought I was being reassuring!" he defended.

"Clearly, we need to work on our communication skills," Kristen pointed out as she stifled a laugh.

Ansel stared at her in bewilderment until the ridiculousness of their situation hit him, too. "We are literally the worst at this," he said, laughing himself.

"It's not really funny," Kristen said between giggles.

"No, it isn't," he replied as he laughed with her. Thankfully, the inappropriate laughter broke the tension between them. "Okay. From this point forward, we will tell each other how we feel and respect one another enough to ask questions and hear each other out before jumping to conclusions. Deal?" he said in a much more serious tone, extending his hand.

She took his hand and shook it. "Deal."

Chapter 11

"Kristen! Ansel! Are the rumors true?!?" They glanced at each other in alarm while working the after-show press line when the reporter with a pert ponytail and tortoiseshell glasses blurted out her question. It had been about a month since they'd found out about the twins, and they were doing all in their power to keep it under wraps. What had this woman found out?

Ansel slipped a casual arm around Kristen's waist. "To what rumors would you be referring?" he asked with a charming smile, trying to deflect attention away from whatever this reporter had discovered. He and Kristen looked quite the pair still in costume. For their performance of the paso doble earlier that evening, she wore a costume resembling an ancient Roman empress, while he was bare-chested and in leather, representing a Roman gladiator.

"That you two are dating! Several sources reported seeing you two around town," the reported informed them, and he inwardly breathed a sigh of relief. Surely, Kristen was feeling the same way. No pregnancy rumors.

Kristen laughed and playfully hit his arm. "Oh no, that isn't true, is it, Ansel?" she piped in, smiling broadly. "We're just really great friends."

He gave her a light squeeze. "The best of friends," he reiterated.

The reporter didn't look convinced, but dropped the matter, spending her precious few minutes with them asking about their dance for the next week and how they felt about their paso doble.

When she'd finished and they made their way to the next reporter, Ansel shot her a look of relief. Her eyes widened briefly and she nodded ever so slightly. No one would even notice their brief, silent exchange, but it was nice to know they were on the same page. With only two weeks of competition left, they'd already had to start getting creative with Kristen's costumes.

Two days earlier, at their wardrobe consult, one of the stylists remarked on Kristen's expanding waistline. Her face had grown red and she'd mumbled something about too many late night bowls of ice cream, but the stylist had looked skeptical.

Other than the teeniest curve developing just below her waist, Kristen really didn't look any different, and no one, save him and clearly their stylist, would even remotely note a change in her size or appearance. Nevertheless, he'd helped come up with the Roman theme for the dance and pushed for the paso doble, which would allow her to have a flowing costume.

"That was mortifying!" she'd whispered after they'd left the wardrobe consult.

"You're carrying twins—we knew we were going to have to get creative—story and costume wise. There's no way you're not going to show at all before this is over."

"But can we get away with baggy costumes?" she asked, arching an eyebrow.

He shook his head. "No, not baggy, just . . . creative—a little flounce or ruffle, maybe a strategically placed drape . . . nothing too crazy."

"Okay, whatever you say. I trust you when it comes to this stuff," she'd relented.

And in her ivory empress costume with a crown of golden leaves settled among her blond-streaked curls and braids, she was beautiful—ethereal even. No one would ever guess they were trying to hide the subtle change to her body. They would only focus on how gorgeous she appeared.

Moving through the press line, they were asked time and again if things were heating up off the dance floor. They answered over and over that they were just friends. By the time they were finished, Kristen stared at him, wide-eyed.

"Hey, Ansel, just friend of mine. We're just friends. Did you know that we're just friends?" she asked cynically.

He rolled his eyes. "I know it gets old, but I'm glad they aren't pushing too hard. And it's not like we aren't telling the truth. Besides, I'm sure someone somewhere has a picture of us—whether from dinner out or holding hands or something that could totally be enough to sell a story about us being in a relationship if we even hinted that to be the case."

"I guess that wouldn't be the end of the world," she admitted, glancing down and fiddling with a fold in her silky gown.

"No, it wouldn't, but it would cause all sorts of scrutiny," he said slowly. What did she mean saying it wouldn't be the end of the world? She was the one that had put the brakes on anything further happening with them romantically. Not that he blamed her at all. A relationship would just complicate the fragile balance they'd managed to find.

She yawned. "I'm so tired, I could fall asleep standin' up," she said, her Southern accent more pronounced than usual. He always noticed it the most when she was tired.

He put an arm around her shoulders and she leaned into him. "Let's get changed," he said softly, leading her outdoors, and in the direction of the cast trailers.

"It's going to take me twenty minutes just to scrub off the five layers of makeup on my face," she complained. "I bet you're wishing you didn't have to wait for me." He had picked her up on his way to the studio earlier that day.

"It's no big deal." He parted ways with her and headed to his trailer to change, realizing he meant it. He really didn't mind waiting for her. Actually, he looked forward to their drive home, going over their dance and just chatting about mundane nothingness. He'd found in her something special—a friend—not a romantic conquest, or just a dance partner, but a true friend.

Chapter 12

"We have to really focus, Kristen. We've only got three more days before the finale," Ansel said as he wiped the sweat beading on his brow.

Kristen struggled to catch her breath. "I know—I'm trying, I swear."

"I know you are. It's just a lot of pressure, you know?" he said before drinking heartily from his water bottle. He eyed Kristen closely. At the sight of the deep circles under her eyes, flushed cheeks and sagging shoulders, a pang of guilt swept through him. The show still didn't have a clue that she was pregnant, thank God, and they certainly weren't aware that it was by his doing. She was trying her best to keep up with their slammed schedule, and it was wreaking havoc on her.

For the last couple of weeks, they'd managed to collaborate and do surprisingly well in the final stages of competition, despite their unique circumstances. They talked very little of the pregnancy, except in terms of Kristen's health and wellness. As far as conversations regarding future plans, their relationship, or the babies, they'd both decided it was best to shelve those topics until after the show officially wrapped.

But now in the studio, as he took in her haggard appearance, he placed a hand of concern on her shoulder, worries about her side turns and heel leads forgotten. "Kristen, are you feeling alright?"

She nodded vigorously. "Yeah, of course. Just a little tired, that's all," she said, catching her breath.

Ansel glanced at the clock then back at her. "Maybe we should go ahead and call it a day."

Kristen's mouth dropped. "No way. We still have two hours of scheduled studio time. There's no way I'm going to let my being tired affect our chances of winning." She grinned fiercely, but Ansel saw the clench of her jaw, the droopiness of her tired eyelids.

He shook his head at her, determined to put his foot down. "You're exhausted, Kristen." He added, his voice a little lower, "You have to take care of yourself."

Her head shot up. "I know that. Don't you think I know that?" Fire blazed in her eyes.

He put both of his hands up in a sign of surrender. "Hey, no need to take offense. I'm just worried about you, that's all. And it's part of my job, may I remind you, to ensure your safety and well-being while you are participating with the show. I really feel that we should cut practice short."

She huffed, blowing a stray lock of hair out of her face as she rolled her eyes. "Let's at least practice for one more hour. That's a compromise, right?"

He studied her, knowing how stubborn she could be—it was in his best interest to concede to her compromise. "Fine. One hour and not a minute more." Even as he said it, he couldn't believe the words had left his mouth. Under normal circumstances and in previous seasons, he had had to practically plead with contestants to rehearse.

"Let's get to it, then," Kristen reaffirmed, tossing her empty bottle to the side and wiping the sweat from her face. Ansel surveyed her grim determination, and despite the nagging feeling that he should still call the practice, he held his arms out for her to step into them.

Everything went smoothly for the duration of practice, but when Ansel asked Kristen if she wanted to grab a quick bite to eat afterward, she yawned heavily.

"I'd be completely fine with that, but I'm too tired to move, much less eat," she admitted.

"You need to eat, Kristen," Ansel reminded gently. "What if I pick something up and bring it over to your apartment?" he suggested.

She shrugged. "That's fine, if you want. You don't have to do that though. I'm sure I can scrounge up a granola bar or something."

He rolled his eyes. "I'll get us a couple of veggie burgers from that diner down the street."

Her eyes lit up. "I love those! I could eat one every day. Will you get the extra pickles I like so much? Dill, not sweet, remember?" she asked, making a face at the memory of the time the diner had put bread and butter pickles on her burger.

He chuckled. "Of course," he said, already pulling out his phone and looking up the diner's number. "I'll be there as soon as I pick up the food."

She placed a hand on his arm. "Thanks, Ansel," she replied with a tired smile before heading to her car. He watched the bounce of her blond-streaked ponytail as she walked away. With her svelte figure and stellar appearance, no one would ever guess that the bubbly young woman was three months pregnant. Well, as long as they didn't study her too closely—loose tank tops did wonders—or visit the studio's ladies' room at precisely 10:30 when morning sickness still struck her at the exact same time each day, no matter what she did or did not have to eat, or happen into her apartment around eight at night when she would already be conked out on the sofa, still holding *What to Expect When You're Expecting* in her lap.

Ansel smiled, his heart doing that funny twitchy thing it tended to do lately when he thought about Kristen. Unsure what it meant, he dialed the restaurant and shook his head, not wanting to dwell on the warm feeling any longer. The weird, strangely intense affection he had for Kristen wasn't part of his plan. He wasn't even thirty yet and had no intentions of settling down for quite some time. The curveball of Kristen getting unexpectedly pregnant and its repercussions weren't issues he was ready to explore just yet. They'd both decided it was best to put off decisions and plans regarding the babies until after the competition ended, which meant he could certainly put off dealing with the foreign feelings he was beginning to have for his dance partner for a few more days, and hopefully, the unnatural affection would just go away altogether by that point. Then, they could make a logical decision, devoid of romantic feelings that clouded judgment, about what was best for the twins on the way. But for now, he had to get his head in the game. He had to focus on winning that trophy. That was all that mattered at the moment, he reminded himself over and over.

***

Half an hour later, he arrived at Kristen's apartment and waited a solid five minutes outside her front door after he'd texted her and knocked a few times. She finally opened it, yawning widely. Little mascara smudges were beneath one of her sleepy blue-green eyes.

"I woke you up, didn't I?" he asked, stepping inside with the aromatic bag of burgers.

"Yeah, but it's my bad for falling asleep when I knew you were on the way. The food smells amazing!" She took the bag from him and padded in her socks to the apartment's galley kitchen. She set to work plating their food while Ansel grabbed a bottle of water from her small fridge, pouring them each a glass.

They ate standing in the kitchen, no ceremony or frills accompanying their evening meal. Ansel noticed that Kristen was unusually quiet.

"Everything okay?" he asked as he rinsed his now empty plate.

She nodded, chewing thoughtfully.

Finished rinsing, he washed his hands and toweled them off, still waiting to see if she said anything. She only continued to finish eating, her eyes focused on her plate.

"Something's wrong," he pointed out, hoping to draw a bit of information out of her.

She wiped her mouth and set her plate in the sink. "Nothing's wrong," she shrugged, heading into the living room and plopping down on the sofa. He followed her, noticing the little curve of her belly when she stretched out comfortably.

"I don't believe you."

Kristen turned to face him as he took a seat on the edge of the sofa near her curled-up feet. "I'm sure you've noticed," she remarked, sweeping a hand across the front of her. He glanced down at her small baby bump.

"I've noticed—it's hard not to when we dance against one another for hours at a time each day, but I know you're pregnant. People that don't know won't notice." He reached out and put a hand over the slight curve. She placed her hand on top of his, but eyed him suspiciously.

"I don't know if I believe you. Charlene has noticed I'm getting fatter."

"As our stylist, it's Charlene's job to notice any changes in your measurements—and you're not getting fatter."

"Yes, I am!" she argued, scrambling to sit up. She shook her head furiously. "I don't want to talk about this. We said we weren't going to talk about this stuff until after the show was over," she said firmly.

"Kristen—"

"NO!" she interrupted. "I mean it. We're not going to talk about it anymore." She grabbed the remote and flipped on the television. He stared at her. The girl was nothing but stubborn.

Hours later, he carried her snoring figure to her bed and tucked her in carefully before making sure her alarm was set for the next morning. After flicking off the lights, save for the light over the oven in the kitchen, he tiptoed out of her darkened apartment, checking twice to make sure the door was locked.

Chapter 13

"I can't believe you just snuck out like that," Kristen grumbled as she stretched her arms. Her shoulders were sore from hours of practicing their last dance together—a Viennese waltz— and her pale peach dress was a little snugger than she would have preferred. She could barely breathe!

"I didn't sneak out," he leaned over and told her. "You were dead to the world, so I put you in your bed, locked up and headed home. Forgive me for taking care of you," he said with sarcasm.

She sighed, annoyed with herself. "Sorry, I'm in such a bad mood—I'm just tired," she mumbled.

"It's okay. Just one more day and it's all over," he reminded her, standing behind her and gently massaging her shoulders. She closed her eyes as he worked at the tense muscles.

"Ansel!" a crew member called, "We need you and Kristen on the floor immediately. Let's go!"

"They're always in such a rush," Kristen remarked as they hurried toward the stairs that led down to the dance floor.

"Everything runs on a tight schedule," Ansel said over his shoulder heading down the steps first.

Love Isn't a Show

Kristen couldn't help but admire the broad set of his shoulders and how handsome he was in his coat and tails. This show really knew how to dress their cast to impress.

She must have been distracted, that's all she could figure when she thought about the incident later. Why else would she have been so careless as to not firmly hold the handrail as she hurried down the studio's steep steps?

Her left foot in its glamorous ballroom heel had missed the step by a few inches, causing her to lose her balance and tumble forward, flipping over and landing hard on her back. Because Ansel had been in front of her, tumbling into him kept her from sliding down several more steps. Thankfully, he didn't lose his own balance at the force of her knocking against the back of his legs.

"Oh, God! Kristen!" Ansel shouted, kneeling on the steps. "Medic! We need a medic!" he cried out, looking down in horror to see her crumpled on the steps.

"Don't say anything about you know," she said under her breath, grimacing in pain.

"What? Kristen, you can't be serious. Where are you hurting? Do you think I can move you?"

"I landed on my back and it really hurts, but I think I can stand," she said, wincing as she tried to move.

"No, stay put just in case you knocked something out of place," he said, worry etched all over his face as they shared a private look. Kneeling awkwardly beside her on the staircase, he held her hand and didn't leave her side as they waited for the paramedics to arrive. As she lay stiffly, still on the steps, her mind turned from the excruciating pain radiating along her lower spine to concern for the itty-bitty babies many months away from being born. She prayed her fall hadn't harmed them in any way. Maybe she hadn't been overly absorbed with the fact that she would be a mother in the past few weeks, but she loved those unborn babies so much already. Her mind ran over stories she'd read on the internet, different articles and blogs about how precarious the first three months were, and even though she had cruised past the three-month mark a few days ago, she was carrying twins, which in and of itself made her pregnancy more of a high-risk situation. What if the fall had injured one or both of them somehow? What if it caused her to miscarry?

Tears coursed down her face, more out of fear than pain, as one of the cameramen hovered nearby, recording the tense situation from as close an angle as possible.

"Can you back it up with that thing? She's really hurt!" Ansel exclaimed to the cameraman when he got a little too close. Lowering his gear, the man gave the seasoned pro a confused look. He was just doing his job.

"How bad is the pain?" Ansel asked her.

"It's bad, but I think I could probably get up, I really do. I'm just . . . scared," she admitted.

"It's best that you don't move. We take back and neck injuries very serious here. The producers will want to make sure all their bases are covered with a full, thorough examination," he told her.

"How thorough?"

"Tons of X-rays, for one."

"Ansel, I don't think I can—"

"They'll need to know your medical history," he told her in code, his eyes wary.

She nodded. "I know, but they can't disclose anything, right? Privacy laws and stuff are in place for a reason."

Just then, two paramedics wheeled a stretcher onto the ballroom floor below them. They left their gear at the foot of the steps and hurried to Kristen. Ansel stepped back to give them room to examine her. They asked her what seemed like a million questions, ranging from if she'd hit her head during the fall to her pain level to what she'd had for breakfast that morning. After their battery of questions, they determined, as Ansel assumed that they would, not to have her stand or move from where she lay. They zoomed back down the steps and grabbed a backboard from their supplies. The two seasoned paramedics managed to slide her onto the board with only minimal pain on her part.

As they carried her down the ten steps or so, her cheeks flushed red in embarrassment. Several cast and crew members were watching, a mix of concern and curiosity on their faces. Why had she been so careless? Ansel waited at the foot of the steps by the stretcher. Once they secured her to the wheeled device, he didn't leave her side as they pushed her outside into the midafternoon heat.

"Sir, we really need to get her to the hospital," the older paramedic with gray at his temples told Ansel once they'd reached the ambulance.

"I'm coming with her," Ansel said firmly.

"Are you family?" he asked.

"Sort of," he said.

"You either are or you aren't."

"She's my fiancée," he blurted out and Kristen's eyes widened from where she lay in the back of the ambulance.

"Hop in, then," the paramedic replied and Ansel jumped up, perching beside her and taking her hand once more. She bit her lip, unsure how to feel about

Love Isn't a Show

Ansel calling her his fiancée. He laid a light hand on her stomach.

"I hope that was okay—because you are my family," he said sincerely.

"Of course," she replied softly as the ambulance lurched forward. She winced as it jarred her injured back.

An hour later, she was settled on a bed in the crowded triage area of the Cedars-Sinai Emergency Room, the flimsy patterned curtain pulled closed, though it afforded little privacy. She'd noticed a few looks of recognition as she'd been wheeled inside, especially since Ansel had yet to leave her side. He was recognized just about everywhere he went.

"What if one of those paramedics tells the wrong person you said you were my 'fiancé'?" she asked, her voice barely above a whisper as she waited to be worked up by a nurse.

Ansel shrugged. "I had to say something that would get me on that ambulance, and I don't think those two guys care much about celebrity gossip. Besides, right now I care more about you and them," his eyes darted to her waist, "than I do about the show or the press."

Something inside of her warmed unexpectedly at his fierce devotion. As she glanced over at the worried man beside her, it was as if she was seeing him for the first time. Gone was the suave, cocky playboy she'd met three months ago. In his place was a concerned, mature man that refused to leave her side. Her heart thudded in her chest, partly from nerves, but also from the feelings she'd pushed down and sealed away that suddenly sprang forth, threatening to burst through her heart all over again.

"Ms. Manning?" A nurse in navy-blue scrubs swung through the curtain, a portable vitals machine with her.

"That's me."

"Your ER registration says that you experienced a fall down a flight of steps today and you're presenting with lower back pain," the nurse, whose nametag read "Helene," read from the tablet she held.

"That's correct."

The nurse typed a few things down, then attached the blood pressure cuff and oximeter to Kristen, waiting for the digital readouts of her vitals to pop up on the machine. Kristen glanced nervously at Ansel.

"Um," Kristen cleared her throat, "I think I should let you know that I'm thirteen weeks pregnant."

The nurse's head shot up. "Oh, okay. Thank you for telling us. That's very important information regarding your treatment." She jotted down a few more notes.

"Have you experienced any pain or cramping in your abdomen?"

"No." Thank the Lord.

"Any spotting?"

"No."

"Who is your obstetrician?"

"Dr. Goldblum."

"Are there any concerns as of yet with your pregnancy?"

"It's not a concern necessarily, but I am carrying twins."

Nurse Helene jotted down even more notes. When she seemed satisfied, she announced, "The doctor will be in with you shortly," before slipping out of the curtained space.

Kristen let out a breath she hadn't realized she'd been holding. A tear, of frustration or fear, she wasn't sure which, slid down her cheek.

"Hey, it's going to be okay," Ansel soothed, squeezing her hand.

"Is it Ansel? I'm not so sure," she said, her voice trembling.

Chapter 14

Ansel glanced down at Kristen, lying tensely on the hospital bed, still wearing her sequined and feathered dress. He'd removed her heels and held them by the straps in the hand that wasn't holding hers. She looked terrified.

Dancers got injured all the time—Kristen wasn't even the first contestant to take a tumble down the stairs at a rehearsal. But never before had he experienced so much fear for someone else, or been in a situation where something so dear to him was on the line and there wasn't a single thing within his own control.

No matter how many times he assured her that everything was going to be alright, it didn't make a difference. They both knew two little lives were on the line and until a medical professional told them everything was fine, neither of them would be able to relax.

Soon after the nurse left, a young man in a lab coat slipped inside the curtained wall. "Hi, Ms. Manning, I'm Dr. Kravich, and I'm the attending physician in the ER today," he said, running over the notes he held in his hand.

"Hi, Dr. Kravich," she said politely.

Love Isn't a Show

"I see here that you suffered a fall and that you are also in the very beginning of your second trimester with twins?"

"That's correct."

Ansel squeezed her hand when she looked up at him with uncertainty.

The doctor glanced between the two of them. "Okay, here's the deal—because you are still in the stages of early pregnancy and the fetuses are not yet viable, we can only treat you in the ER for your back injury. However, we have called Dr. Goldblum, who is the on-call ob-gyn right now anyway, and she said she would come in and examine you as a precautionary matter. Thankfully, you aren't experiencing pain, cramping, or spotting, so the likelihood of miscarriage is low."

"Even though you call them unviable, my babies are the most important thing here to me. I don't want any treatment that will compromise their health," Kristen said vehemently.

"I would strongly suggest you have an X-ray done. A single X-ray will be of minimal risk to your babies' health, but if you have an injury to your back and it isn't treated, that could cause greater harm to you and them in the long run."

"O-okay," she agreed. "Is Dr. Goldblum on her way?"

"She should be here within the hour," the doctor assured. "A tech will be here shortly to take you to radiology."

"Doctor? Please keep the pregnancy information as confidential as you can. We don't want anyone finding out."

"Our patients' privacy is of the utmost importance to us while they are being treated here. Your condition will be known only when it is imperative to your treatment." With those words, he left them.

"Ansel," she said, turning to him and clutching his hand, "I can't believe I tried to put off thinking about the babies these past few weeks. I feel so guilty," she admitted, tears welling in her eyes again.

"What are you talking about, Kristen?" he asked incredulously. "Sure, maybe we haven't talked in detail about what we're going to do after the show, but you've been a great mother already. You're always exercising, eating healthy and reading up on how to have a healthy baby. You haven't drunk a cup of coffee in weeks. Don't feel guilty," he said fiercely. If anyone had reason to feel guilty, it was him. He was the one that had put her here—changed her life forever, all the while trying so hard to pretend that they didn't have to talk about it.

"You shouldn't feel guilty either," she murmured, as if reading his mind. "You have been an amazing friend these past few weeks—and you're always watching out for me and being incredibly attentive. I haven't doubted once that you really care about them," she said, glancing down at her stomach, her hand subconsciously resting over it, as if to protect her precious cargo from the outside world.

"Because I do, Kristen . . . and I care about you, too," he told her. He wanted to say so much more, but for some reason, the words stuck in his throat.

"Ms. Manning? I'm here to take you down to radiology," an orderly announced, peeling back the curtain panel. The younger woman's eyes widened to see the two of them, still in costume and holding hands.

"So the rumors are true," she mumbled under her breath.

"We're just friends," Kristen corrected the girl, promptly removing her hand from Ansel's. His hand felt empty and cool now. Why did it bother him so much to hear her say that?

"Oh, sorry. None of my business anyway," the orderly's cheeks bloomed pink and she shrugged her shoulders at the recognition of her blunder. She turned her attention to Ansel. "You can wait here—she'll only be gone for a few minutes," she explained.

Ansel nodded and watched Kristen being wheeled away, sitting awkwardly in the wheelchair. He wished he could have gone with her, even for something as simple as a quick X-ray.

While she was gone, he pulled his cellphone out and typed a quick message to Elaine, a member of the *Dance With Me* production staff.

Kristen is being X-rayed now. Will be a while before we get results. I'll keep you posted-Ansel.

He slipped the phone back in his pocket, not really caring when or if he received a response from Elaine. All he cared about was Kristen and their babies at the moment. He sat pensively on the edge of Kristen's empty bed. As he stared at the speckled, glossy floor, he couldn't believe how much his life had changed in such a short amount of time. Barely three months ago, he spent most nights out and about, a beautiful woman always ready and willing to spend those nights with him. He wasn't a relationship or commitment kind of guy. Truth be told, he had never planned on settling down. Why would he?

Plenty of money, fame and his looks had seemed to be enough for him. His parents, married for almost 35 years, lived a quiet life. Up until recently, he'd always considered them tired and boring. But now, as he thought of the secret smiles they tended to share, or the way his father held his mother's hand whenever they were out and about, he saw things differently. They shared a love and bond that he craved. With Kristen.

He was in love with Kristen.

He ran his hands through his hair, sighing heavily as the realization hit him. A relationship with him was probably the last thing on Kristen's mind. He'd hurt her so many times over the past three months. Sure, he'd been trying to make up for it recently, but she'd been adamant that they just be friends while they competed. He'd respected her wishes.

Just then, the orderly pushed Kristen in a wheelchair back into the semi-private space.

"That was quick," he remarked as the orderly helped Kristen back onto the bed. Kristen gave him a slight smile as she settled in and tried to get comfortable while they waited for Dr. Goldblum and the results of her X-ray.

Twenty minutes later, Dr. Goldblum bustled in, wearing a surgical cap and dark green scrubs. "Hi, Kristen. I don't have but a minute—I'm on my way to perform a C-section upstairs, but I looked at your chart. You don't have any symptoms that would suggest a risk of miscarriage, but I've ordered an ultrasound, just to make sure everything is as it should be," she said briskly.

"Thank you so much, Dr. Goldblum," Kristen said, relieved to hear some sort of news regarding the twins.

"You're welcome. I'll be down to go over the results as soon as I'm out of surgery," she said with a nod, hurrying off to deliver another baby.

Not even five minutes later, another orderly, this time an older woman with long braids, came to collect Kristen for her ultrasound. "Want to come with me?" Kristen asked Ansel.

"May I?" Ansel asked, glancing at the orderly.

"Sure," the orderly responded warmly. He followed along as the orderly pushed Kristen down the hall to a quiet, private room. The overhead lights were off, and a computer screen illuminated the shadowy space. Another woman in pink scrubs sat at the computer.

"Hello, I'm Marcia, the ultrasound tech performing your sonogram today," the woman at the computer stood and said.

"Hi, I'm Kristen, and this is my friend, Ansel," Kristen said nervously. The orderly helped her onto the cushioned examination table before exiting with the wheelchair.

"So, according to your chart, you're roughly thirteen weeks pregnant with twins. Why don't we take a look?" She smiled warmly.

Kristen glanced down at her attire—not really suitable for a medical procedure. Marcia noticed her concerns.

"I'll give you a gown and a sheet to change into," she explained, pulling a flimsy gown and a folded paper sheet from a drawer and handing it to Kristen. She then directed her to the bathroom inside the small room.

"Do you need help changing?" Ansel asked her. She looked up at him and warily nodded her head. She hadn't received the results from her X-ray yet and was trying to move as minimally as possible.

He scooped her up and carried her into the bathroom. She held herself up against the wall as he unzipped her dress and pulled it over her head. She squeezed her eyes shut in embarrassment that wasn't really warranted. He'd seen her naked quite a few times before. But almost instantly, he helped her slide her arms through the thin, cotton gown and buttoned what he could in the back.

"There, all done," he said, folding the gown over his arm carefully before lifting her again and returning her to the examination table.

Kristen unfolded the sheet, spreading it across her legs and lifted the gown as she was instructed. She tucked the paper around her hips as Ansel averted his eyes politely because even though he'd just helped her change, and they'd slept together a handful of times, they were just friends now. Just friends having children together.

Love Isn't a Show

Marcia squirted a warm, jellylike substance over her exposed skin before positioning the ultrasound wand firmly, moving in slow, steady strokes as she watched the screen intently. Ansel stared, too, concentrating on what, he wasn't sure.

Within seconds, the rapid heartbeat of one of the babies filled the room. The fluttering sounded like music to Kristen's ears and she sighed in blissful relief. Ansel watched as the perfect little profile of a baby appeared on the screen.

"This is Baby A," Marcia stated, clicking a few buttons to capture shots of the baby as she moved the wand around. Ansel's heart tightened at the sight of the baby on the screen. It didn't look like an alien blob anymore—the picture showed a full profile from its little nose to its stretched-out legs.

"And here is Baby B," Marcia said, as the sound of another heartbeat filled the room. Baby B wasn't quite as cooperative for pictures, as it was facing the other direction.

Kristen slipped her hand into Ansel's as tears threatened to fall for the ten thousandth time that afternoon. From her previous doctor's visit that had included an ultrasound, Kristen knew that since Marcia was just a tech, she didn't have the authority to tell them that the babies were healthy, but she knew enough to know that if something was wrong,

Marcia would have gotten up and hurried to find a doctor immediately.

"That's our babies," she whispered to Ansel, squeezing his hand. "Our perfect little babies."

Chapter 15

"I can walk without any help from you, Ansel," Kristen complained, tired, irritable and hungry after spending over six hours in the emergency room.

"That doesn't mean I don't *want* to help you," he replied calmly as they walked to her building's elevator.

She sighed in frustration, her back still aching as they waited for the slow elevator. "I'm fine to compete tomorrow."

He arched an eyebrow at her. "I don't know, Kristen . . ."

"The doctor said it was fine as long as I'm careful, which I promise, I will be." Why was she having to even talk him into this? It was *the finals* for crying out loud! If they didn't dance, they were finished. No trophy, but worse than that, no prize money. Taking care of two newborns wasn't going to be cheap, and she hadn't come this far to lose now.

"I know that, but it still poses some risk. I don't know what I would do if you got hurt, not to mention the twins." Worry lines creased around his eyes.

She admired his concern—based on everything she'd known about him up until the last couple of weeks, it was utterly out of character for him to care about anything other than himself or winning. So he seriously needed to get on board with continuing to compete. "I'm fine, Ansel. We're dancing a waltz—no crazy tricks or anything, just a beautiful, traditional Viennese waltz. I think I can handle it."

Kristen trudged into her apartment, tugging on the loose blue scrubs a kind ER tech had given her to wear instead of that drafty hospital gown or her ballroom dress, which Ansel now carried inside for her. All she wanted to do was collapse on her sofa and fall asleep, but she needed a good, hot shower first. "Hang that over there," she gestured to coat rack on the wall.

"Actually, I'm going to take it to wardrobe first thing in the morning so they can steam it for you, if that's alright."

She smiled, softening. "Of course, thank you."

He nodded, turning to leave.

"Ansel, wait," she called out, lifting a hand.

He turned expectantly.

She took a deep breath. "Do you mind staying here tonight? I don't want to be alone just in case . . ." she trailed off. She didn't want to say her deepest fears out loud. The potential threat of miscarriage still hung heavy on her mind.

"I don't mind at all," he replied, hanging up the dress and closing the distance between them. He took both of her hands in his. "I'll always be here for you," he said tenderly. She swallowed, overwhelmed by the gentle look in his eyes, and the way his thumbs ran slowly back and forth across the tops of her hands. In that moment, beneath his gaze, she felt safe—she felt at home.

Squeezing her eyes shut, she pulled her hands from his. "Great. Awesome. There's some extra blankets in my bedroom, and the couch is really comfy," she stammered, her voice shaking. Ansel did something to her, made her feel things she wasn't ready to feel, and that wasn't something she was prepared to handle. She had to focus. They had to win. There were babies on the way. He wasn't known for being in a committed relationship. She didn't want him to hurt her again.

"Kristen," Ansel started, confused. "Are you alright?"

"Yes, of course! I'm just tired, and I need a shower after sitting in that germ-filled waiting room," she told him, backing out of the room and shutting her bathroom door firmly behind her. She took a few deep breaths, trying to calm her thudding heart. She willed her wayward emotions to get back in check. This was not the time to be weak!

She slumped against the door, tears welling in her eyes. Oh, but wasn't it though? She'd never been more scared in her entire life than she was when she'd fallen down the steps earlier today, and it certainly hadn't been for herself. She'd been terrified that she might have lost the two babies she already loved, even if she had yet to meet them.

Her hand fluttered to her belly, knowing somewhere within, two sweet little ones were still safe and sound. But she'd been terrified of losing them because of her fall. That's why she'd asked Ansel to stay with her, knowing for all of his faults, he'd proven that he cared greatly for his children already. He understood her fear—they'd both been scared when she fell, and that feeling wasn't easy to shake.

If she could just get her crazy emotions under control, she could concentrate on the next two days. The following night, they would perform their final dance for the judges, and then the next night, the winning couple would be announced. Only three couples remained in the competition, and one would be eliminated tomorrow night after their performances. Kristen prayed it wouldn't be her and Ansel. They'd come too far and gone through too much not to make it all the way.

Love Isn't a Show

***

Ansel stared at Kristen's closed bathroom door. He wanted to barge in, take her in his arms and tell her exactly what he felt. That yes, of course he cared about their twins. Of course, he would always be there for the mother of his children. But also, he was completely in love with her and he was utterly wrecked without her. He wanted her, no needed her, in his life. Always.

But, instead of saying all that, he just stared at the door, his hands in fists by his side. With a frustrated sigh, he choked down the words and turned, plopping down on the sofa to wait for her return.

He'd always prided himself on being confident, suave and an absolute ladies' man. But when it came to this particular woman, his stomach was in knots. She'd been adamant she only wanted to be friends, and he didn't want to overstep the strict boundaries she'd put in place. However, he'd never felt this way about anyone in his entire life. He wanted to shout his love for her from the rooftops, but instead found himself unable to vocalize a single word to her in reference to it.

Sure, he had no problem telling her he cared about her. Or expressing his concern for her, or his love for their unborn children. But when it came to the heart-pounding, palms-sweating, ridiculous love he had in his heart for her, his lips froze and his tongue felt like lead in his mouth. He wanted to tell her, he did. He just had to gather the gumption to do it.

Chapter 16

The following night in the televised ballroom, Ansel took Kristen into his arms for what was surely the thousandth time. Although the feel of her was incredibly familiar and seemed completely natural, this was their last official dance, which gave the moment a bittersweet air. This was the last time he would whirl her around the dance floor as millions of viewers watched. In seasons past, he would be wound tightly though appearing totally at ease, but this season, things were different. With eyes only for her, he led her with a calmness he'd never known through the graceful dance, admiring her perfect form, the elegant lines of her lithe neck, the gentle expression on her face. He could tell she was concentrating on each step, but trying to make her face appear soft and romantic. He bit back a grin.

As she leaned back in his arms and balanced on one foot, he spun her around while the pale peach dress rippled in the breeze. Pulling her back firmly against him, he caught her eyes briefly, willing himself not to get lost in the blue-green depths. In front of all these people as they were being judged on their performance was not the time to tell her he was hopelessly in love with her.

But oh, how he wanted to do just that. It was all he could think about. Not three-quarter turns or box steps. He was focused on keeping his lips clamped shut because "I love you" kept wanting to burst out of them.

Like, right then, as the music ended and he dipped her dramatically back and she was grinning up at him, relieved to be finished, euphoric from the crowd's energy and their perfectly executed dance. Her eyes shone, her nose wriggled.

"I love you, Kristen," he blurted out as he gazed down at her beautiful face, unable to keep it to himself any longer. All the chaos surrounding them didn't matter. Her mouth popped open in surprise before giving way to a radiant smile of pure joy.

"Oh Ansel, I love you, too. I really do," she said breathlessly. He stared down at her for a brief second more before leaning down and brushing her lips tenderly with his own. The crowd erupted with cheers, but he didn't care. The only thing that mattered was the beautiful creature in his arms who had just made him the happiest man alive.

However, the show had to go on, and so he lifted his head from hers, and straightened, helping her stand upright in the process. They hurried over to the platform in front of the judges' booth, where Jerry, the show's host awaited them.

"Wow, that was some ending," Jerry kidded them, to the audience's delight. Ansel may have been caught up in the moment when he kissed her, but now, beneath the blaring spotlights with a microphone shoved in his face, reality sunk back in, and the last thing he wanted was to exploit his and Kristen's delicate relationship to the world.

He cleared his throat. "Sometimes, when you dance such a beautiful dance with a beautiful lady, you get caught up in the moment," he said, shrugging carelessly.

Jerry arched a skeptical eyebrow at him, but pried no further—everyone in the audience and on the show knew his reputation with the ladies. "Let's see the judges' scores," he said, gesturing towards the elevated screen.

Much to his delight, a perfect score popped onto the screen. He pulled Kristen into a tight hug as they thanked the judges and begged the at-home viewers to call in and vote for them one last time before hurrying backstage.

With his arm still around Kristen, they headed toward the door that led to the trailers outside. Another couple had to dance and then a female troupe ensemble was performing, plus a couple of commercial breaks were scheduled before they were due back on set.

Kristen hadn't really said anything since they left the stage. "Are you alright?" he asked as they burst through the doors leading outside.

She turned to him, a smile pasted in place. "Sure, why wouldn't I be?"

"You're not alright. What's wrong?"

They reached her trailer. "I'm just tired and my back's sore. That's all."

"Let's go inside and I'll massage it like the doctor suggested," he replied.

"You don't have to do that."

"I want to help you—I love you."

Her eyes widened. "So that wasn't just being caught up in the moment?" she squeaked.

He shook his head. "No, of course not, Kristen. I said that about the kiss because I didn't want the world to start prying into our personal lives. I meant what I said," he told her, shifting on the flimsy metal stair outside of her trailer as she stood leaning out the doorway, "I am completely, 100 percent in love with you. There's no one else for me in this life but you, and I've known that all along, I think, but I didn't realize it fully until about two days ago."

Kristen pulled him inside and the door shut behind them. She threw her arms around his neck. "Oh, Ansel," she said quietly, "I love you, too. I was afraid of it—afraid of getting hurt mainly, but I can't deny how I feel any longer."

"I won't hurt you, Kristen. I know I have in the past and I am so sorry. I feel terrible about it, but I've changed. You've changed me. You mean more to me than anything. Wherever you are, is where I want to be—I'll even relocate to . . . Alabama if that's what it takes."

She laughed. "It's not as bad as you make it out to be down there, but I've been toying with the idea of moving to LA for the past few weeks. UCLA's master's program is amazing, and I've only got a couple of semesters left. I don't want the babies to be shuffled back and forth across the country all the time anyway," she told him.

"Really? You would move here?" he asked, trying not to sound too ecstatic. To have Kristen here would mean so much—he would be near his love and their children, he could keep his job, his parents would get to see their grandchildren more often, they could look for a house together in the suburbs—his mind was reeling with all of the wonderful possibilities.

"Yes, I really would—as long as we sit down and determine that that is the best course of action," she answered, her tone serious. He nodded silently before scooping her up in his arms and kissing her until they were both gasping for breath.

Chapter 17

The next morning after their whirlwind final dance, Kristen slipped from Ansel's bed while he was still sleeping. The overcast morning sky made it seem much earlier than it really was. In the silent, still apartment, the padding of her bare feet across the wooden floors echoed loudly as she shuffled to the kitchen for a glass of water. It was hard to believe today was the day. That evening, they would find out if they won. With only two couples left, them and surprisingly, Noah Hart and his partner, Elysia, it was down to the wire.

She bit her lip as she poured water into a glass. It would really make moving to LA a thousand times easier if they won. She could use the prize money to settle into an apartment and live off the rest while she finished school and prepared for the birth of her children. She really didn't want to ask Ansel for help. Their relationship was so new, and the whole thing felt awkward.

"Morning," his gruff, sleepy voice called out as he stretched in the bedroom's doorway, wearing only a pair of sleeping shorts.

"Good morning," she replied softly, taking a sip of water. He walked up behind her and put his arms

Love Isn't a Show

around her waist, nuzzling her neck. She sighed at the delicious feeling.

"Come back to bed," he murmured.

"I have to get going—we have a jam-packed day," she reminded him, though she was sorely tempted to slip back between the sheets with him for a little while longer. It had been too long since she'd felt the heat of his kisses on her skin, the length of his body spread out across hers—she surely hadn't had her fill just yet. But they had responsibilities. They had a trophy to win. She shook her head, trying to shake the temptation he offered away, as well.

"We have to be on set so early today—you know that," she pointed out, dislodging herself from his arms. "There'll be plenty of time tonight . . . and tomorrow . . . and the day after that for us to spend time together," she said with a wink.

He sighed. "I'm counting on it. Although, if we win, we'll have a ton of interviews and press appearances to make over the next week," he informed her.

She nodded as she headed back to the bedroom to collect her clothes and change out of his T-shirt she wore. When she bustled back out after changing into the tank top and yoga pants she'd worn over, he was standing at the coffee machine. She gave him a quick kiss.

"I'll see you at the studio, okay?" she reaffirmed before ducking out the door.

***

With the final results show to declare the winner looming later that evening, dressed in a belted evening gown with an embroidered, sequined top and a flowing chiffon skirt, Kristen felt like a princess. That could've possibly been credited to the gold and pearl wreath that adorned her braided and curled locks. Whatever the reason, she felt more beautiful than she had in her entire life, and the ever-growing baby bump she sported was concealed elegantly beneath the full chiffon skirt.

"You look like a goddess," Ansel whispered in her ear as he gave her a hug in greeting. With so many crew members milling about, he didn't kiss her, but the warmth of his words felt intimate against her ear. She shivered.

"Thank you," she said, smiling secretively at him before she took his arm and they made their way to the press line to do a dozen interviews before the live taping began.

***

"The moment you've all been waiting for has finally arrived," Jerry spoke ominously into the microphone. "It's time to announce the winner of this season of *Dance With Me*!"

Love Isn't a Show

Kristen squeezed Ansel's hand, and he shot her a reassuring look. No matter what happened, he was fine either way. If they won, that would be amazing, but if they didn't, he still had her, and having Kristen in his life was a far better thing than winning a competition anyway. And it wasn't like he needed the money—he had plenty of that, thanks to his previous wins, salary as a cast member and paid appearances and sponsorships. Not to mention his investments in his family's ship building business, which he also stood to inherit one day. Money was the least of his concerns. He wanted to win for winning's sake, and also because Kristen wanted it so badly.

After a long, pregnant pause, complete with ominous, suspenseful music, courtesy of the show's extremely talented in-house orchestra, Jerry spoke into his microphone, "And your winners, by a landslide vote, are none other than Kristen Manning and her professional dance partner, Ansel Stavros!"

Kristen was sure her heart had stopped beating. Had Jerry really just announced her and Ansel as the winners? She was pushed forward by Ansel's guiding hand on her back as metallic confetti rained down from the high studio ceiling. They shook hands good-naturedly with Noah and Elysia before Ansel scooped her up and whirled around with her in his arms. She squeezed his neck as adrenaline and joy pulsed through every vein in her body.

"We won!" she exclaimed in wonder. Ansel looked up at her with adoration shining in his eyes.

"Yes, beautiful girl, we certainly did," he replied, his voice thick with emotion and so much meaning. She rested her forehead on his.

"Even better than winning is getting to be with you for the rest of my life," he promised her as the chatter and music faded around them.

"Right back at you, my love," she whispered back.

Epilogue

One Year Later...

The sleek Stavros family yacht bobbed ever so slightly in the Pacific Ocean's gentle waves as the sun began to sink below the horizon. Kristen fussed with the pearls around her neck, a Stavros family heirloom, and nervously smoothed the simple white gown she wore for the hundredth time.

"I never thought you would be a nervous bride," her mother said, smiling as happy tears welled in her eyes. She kissed Kristen's cheek and left so that one of Ansel's cousins could escort her down the aisle to her seat. Kristen took a deep breath as the string quartet began playing the first notes of Mendelssohn's "Wedding March."

As she came out of the captain's quarters, clutching her bouquet of blush pink peonies, she positioned herself to walk down the aisle, and that's when she caught her handsome groom's eye. Right then, all anxiety and fear dissipated. Waiting at the end of the aisle was her beloved, all smiles, and beside him, held by Ansel's father and grandfather, were their twin boys. Nick, held by Papa Stavros, was looking around curiously and kicking his little feet, clad in the cutest little baby boat shoes beneath his tiny linen suit. His brother, Aaron, slept soundly in his great-grandfather's arms.

She walked as if on a cloud to her future. The man before her was not only her love, he was her best friend and a wonderful father to their precious boys. It had only made sense to say yes when he asked her at Christmas to marry him. She'd moved into his apartment promptly after that, but they'd decided to put off the wedding until after the babies were born. Now, their happy, healthy boys were nearly four months old and the spitting image of their father.

Kristen reached the end of the aisle and took Ansel's arm. He leaned over and pressed a soft kiss to her temple before the minister began the ceremony. As he spoke, Kristen's heart warmed. Never in a million years had she imagined how drastically her life would change in such a short amount of time. Her highest aspirations had been to get her degree, settle in a decent apartment and get a job teaching drama.

Thanks to Ansel's help and support with the twins, she would be graduating from the master's program at UCLA after the fall semester, just one semester later than she had originally planned; she was marrying the man of her dreams, and they already had the most amazing children who held her heart fiercely in their chubby, little hands. And when they were older, maybe she would get around to teaching a drama class or two.

Love Isn't a Show

But for now, as her veil danced in the sea breeze, her groom occasionally glanced at her with an adoring look, and her little Nick babbled beside them while his brother snoozed, nothing could have made her more content. She considered herself the luckiest of all women and a silent prayer of thankfulness was in her heart as the minister began reciting the vows that would bind her to her beloved Ansel forever.

What to read next?

If you liked this book, you will also like *The Weekend Girlfriend*. Another interesting book is *Two Reasons to Be Single*.

The Weekend Girlfriend

Jessica has worked hard to be the paralegal that hotshot, sexy attorney Kyle needs. Unfortunately he doesn't see her as just his paralegal but also his own personal assistant. When he blames her for a mix-up in his personal life, Jessica sees no other option but to quit, thinking that her time with him is over. Much to her surprise, Kyle makes a proposition to her that she never thought she would hear coming from his lips. He needs a temporary girlfriend for his sister's wedding and he wants her to be that person. Jessica accepts the challenge and finds herself thrown into his world, learning things about him she never knew. The more time she spends with him outside of work, the more she is drawn to Kyle. As the wedding draws near, she finds herself fighting off some strong feelings for the man. When the wedding weekend is over, will Jessica be able to walk away from Kyle with her heart intact?

Two Reasons to Be Single

Olivia Parker has a job doing what she loves, a wonderful family and plenty of friends, but no luck in the love department. Tired of worrying about it, she decides to swear off love completely and focus on all the good things in her life. Just as she makes her firm resolution, Jake Harper arrives in town and knocks her plans into a tailspin. As the excited single ladies of Morning Glory surround the extremely attractive newcomer, Olivia steers clear of the "casserole brigade," as she calls the women, and tries to keep her distance from Jake. Instead, a variety of situations throw them together and they get to know each other better. They both have reasons for not wanting to get involved in a relationship, but the chemistry between them ignites, even as they desperately attempt to keep it at bay. As things heat up between Olivia and Jake, there is an aura of mystery about him that leaves Olivia certain that he is hiding something. When Jake disappears for a few days without telling Olivia that he is going out of town, she hates the way it makes her feel, and it reminds her of why she was giving up on dating in the first place. As Olivia's feelings for Jake grow, so does the need to find out what exactly brought him to Morning Glory and what he's been hiding.

About Emily Walters

Emily Walters lives in California with her beloved husband, three daughters, and two dogs. She began writing after high school, but it took her ten long years of writing for newspapers and magazines until she realized that fiction is her real passion. Emily likes to create a mental movie in her reader's mind about charismatic characters, their passionate relationships and interesting adventures. When she isn't writing romantic stories, she can be found reading a fiction book, jogging, or traveling with her family. She loves Starbucks, Matt Damon and Argentinian tango.

One Last Thing…

If you believe that *Love Isn't a Show* is worth sharing, would you spend a minute to let your friends know about it?

If this book lets them have a great time, they will be enormously grateful to you – as will I.

Emily

www.EmilyWaltersBooks.com